# IT HAPPENED ON ALLAGASH LAKE

*A Perspective of Life in America and Hope for the Future*

By

John M. Hamilton

© 2024 John M. Hamilton. All rights reserved.

No part of this publication may be reproduced, distributed, or transmitted in any form or by any means, including photocopying, recording, or other electronic or mechanical methods, without the prior written permission of the Publisher; ParkerPublishers and Author; John M. Hamilton, except in the case of brief quotations embodied in critical reviews and certain other noncommercial uses permitted by copyright law.

For permission requests, write to the Author at the address below.

John M. Hamilton

# DEDICATION

Writing a novel, even a fiction novel, is a daunting undertaking. I decided to write this book because, although it's fictitious, it addresses many of the glaring situations existing in our country today.

First, I want to dedicate it to my five children, who are the sole reason I was able to push through the most tumultuous times in my life. They are my everything and have all given an old man more pride and joy than I deserve.

Next, I'd like to dedicate this book to my brothers and sisters from the military and federal law enforcement services.

Finally, I want to offer my sincere appreciation to Mr. Jim White. Jim is a friend who, throughout the writing, provided support and encouragement. Over the year that it took me to pen these words, I often felt like giving up, but Jim always convinced me that it was an important effort and that it needed to be completed. Thanks, Jim!

# PREFACE

"It Happened on Allagash Lake" blends fiction with the reality of today's world, highlighting the challenges we face as a society. Through the journey of Mac, you'll explore themes of division, hope, and the search for clarity in the wilderness of Maine.

This book aims to inspire reflection on our shared values and the potential for unity in turbulent times. Thank you for joining me on this journey.

*John M. Hamilton*

# Table of Contents

CHAPTER 1 The Fight ................................................................. 1
CHAPTER 2 Planning the Trip ..................................................... 7
CHAPTER 3 Travel to The Lake ................................................. 14
CHAPTER 4 Down the Stream ................................................... 24
CHAPTER 5 The Campsite ........................................................ 29
CHAPTER 6 The Adventure Begins ........................................... 33
CHAPTER 7 Day 1 .................................................................... 49
CHAPTER 8 Day 2 .................................................................... 61
CHAPTER 9 Leaving the Lake ................................................... 75
CHAPTER 10 Back to Nebraska ................................................ 93
CHAPTER 11 Financing Solved ................................................. 98
CHAPTER 12 Off to The Cape ................................................. 105
CHAPTER 13 Up to Maine ....................................................... 119
CHAPTER 14 Out to Montana .................................................. 125
CHAPTER 15 Headed to Virginia .............................................. 134
CHAPTER 16 Back to Maine .................................................... 143
CHAPTER 17 Chemquasabamticook Lake ............................... 154
CHAPTER 18 Back to Presque Isle and Beyond ...................... 164
CHAPTER 19 Back to Nebraska and then the Wedding ............ 172
CHAPTER 20 The Wedding, then the Speech .......................... 180
CHAPTER 21 The Campaign Airs ............................................ 188
CHAPTER 22 The Campaign Continues .................................. 199
CHAPTER 23 The Election ...................................................... 205
ABOUT THE AUTHOR ............................................................ 214

# CHAPTER 1
## THE FIGHT

"You fucking Nazi, Trump is gone, and your guns will be gone soon!" It had been some time since the 2020 election, and tensions in the United States were boiling along party lines. The country was suffering a division that was as serious as what existed just prior to the Civil War. A significant representation of the Republican Party absolutely believed that the 2020 election was fraught with irregularities to cause reasonable doubt as to its validity, and an equally significant population of Democrats were still reeling from the results of the 2016 election and the recent attack on the Capital on January 6, 2021. The summer of 2020 saw violence in our streets like we have never seen before, and some state authorities rewarded these activities despite the horrific damage that was being inflicted on private businesses and innocent civilians. An increasing cry was sounded to defund the police and eliminate existing federal law enforcement agencies, even though these professionals serve to protect the American populous. There had been several police shootings of black men, and a few were egregious violations of police training and human decency. It was these actions of a minuscule number of police officers that, at least on the surface, had spawned the riots and destruction. The fact is that most law enforcement professionals are good men and women of all races who work for low wages and endure dangerous work conditions. Answering a call to duty seemed lost to many. Regardless of your stance on the issues we face as a nation, the fact is that we are dangerously divided and desperately in need of healing and coming together as Americans. We live in volatile, dangerous times.

Having served for eighteen years in uniformed service followed by years in federal law enforcement, Mac had no interest in engaging the loudmouthed civilian who was accosting him now. The guy was drunk on alcohol and the fever that is sweeping our country. Mac continued backing away from the aggressor, saying, "We don't need to do this. I'm leaving." But the hot-tempered man was persistent and continued to follow and push Mac. It became clear that the situation was not going to be diffused, and there didn't appear to be a safe way to avoid a physical conflict by continued distancing.

Instinct took over, and Mac, not a large guy, standing around 5'9", spun to face the hostile aggressor. Although Mac isn't a big man, his well-muscled frame (absent the typical beer belly that generally presents in men his age) or maybe his icy, cold blue-steel eyes usually say, "Don't push me" to sober men. Then, a drunk can't be counted on to understand much of anything, much less exhibit any degree of perceptiveness.

The crowded bar opened around the two men, as it seemed to do when a fight was about to break out. Before Mac could utter another warning, the much larger man threw the first punch. Mac easily parred the clumsy attack and stepped into his opponent, wrapping the punching arm in his own left arm, and dropping him, hard, to the floor with a left hip throw. Now, Mac had control of the situation, and the stunned guy was incapacitated. He attempted to get back up, but Mac simply exerted more pressure on the right elbow, which was now in a nice arm bar position. "Dude, it's over," Mac spoke calmly but in a tone that demanded immediate compliance. Throughout the entire fracas, Mac was paying detailed attention to the actions of the aggressor's buddies and recognized that three men appeared ready to step in to help their friend. "Let it go, boys," Mac demanded, "or your buddy goes to the hospital, and then I get really upset!"

Something in Mac's actions, or maybe his voice commands, convinced the group to cease any further assault, and they resorted to loud, boisterous talk but at an increasingly safe distance. "If I let you go, will you let me walk away?" Mac asked his defeated opponent. Reluctantly, the downed man agreed, and Mac released his grip and backed away. He walked out of the bar and directly to his truck in the parking lot, acutely aware of every movement near him as he left.

Mac settled into his truck and drew a long, deep breath. *What the fuck is wrong with us as a people*, he wondered. The whole incident began because Mac had been discussing the right to own and bear arms in America and the responsibility that accompanies that right with a few men that he just met that evening. The discussion was quiet and personal. There was absolutely no intention to enrage anyone with a different perspective on the subject. It was just bar talk. Unfortunately, the big guy who ultimately engaged Mac did hear part of the conversation and didn't like what he heard. He interrupted the group talking with Mac and bellowed that right-wing, gun-toting anarchists were evil and needed to be eliminated from our society. It was because Mac was the first to clarify that he and the other men had no intention of starting trouble, and that the conversation was meant to be among them that was why he was singled out for the fight.

The whole incident disturbed Mac terribly, and he couldn't stop thinking that we were headed for serious trouble when a few guys couldn't have a respectful conversation in a bar without being physically attacked for having an opinion that they were not attempting to impose on anyone else. He was decompressing and drifting into deeper thoughts while the cool spring air flowing through the open window of his truck transported him to a better place and time.

Mac recalled his time in the backwoods of Maine as a younger man. While still in uniformed service, he was stationed in northern Maine with the United States Air Force. Although he had deployed globally at different times, he spent most of his eighteen years living in a place the way it's supposed to be. He was a Master Maine Hunting and Fishing Guide and a competent longline trapper in those days. Many days and nights were spent alone in the back country, where life seemed to be reasonable. It was a hard life, but alone in the woods, Mac learned to see nature for what it was. Without the interference of man, nature chugged along nicely. There was birth, life, and death but it all seemed to occur in harmony and with reason. The weather could be magnificently beautiful or lethally threatening, but it always came full circle in the end. He enjoyed a peace in the backwoods that he never experienced anywhere else.

Mac, nostalgically, wondered if life was really that good in the past or if it was just his own fantasy of something beautiful. He drifted away again, and memories of his children and the great times they enjoyed together in the outdoors flooded his mind. From the time they were able to join him, Mac had often brought either one or all of his three kids on outings with him. He taught them to survive in the deep forests and cedar swamps of Maine, but, more importantly, he taught them to slow down and take in the majesty of nature. They learned to respect the woods, the water, the weather, and the animals that all composed this magnificent symphony of life. By ten years of age, each of his kids was an accomplished outdoorsman (or outdoorsperson, as we would say today). In the process of learning to live with nature, they were taught to be equally respectful and tolerant of other people. Mac used to tell them, "You can't avoid people any more than you can avoid the risks of the woods, but if you offer them the same respect and understanding, then most of the time things will work out ok."

Having recently retired from federal law enforcement, for the first time in his life Mac had more time on his hands than he knew what to do with. The events of the evening and his thoughts about a calmer, more understandable time and place made the decision an easy one. He was headed back to one of his favorite places in the world to regroup and unwind. He figured that he would start planning a month-long trip to Allagash Lake, Maine, in the morning. The Chevy engine roared to life and Mac headed home to get some rest and prepare for his trip. Politics and all the national craziness would just have to wait for a while.

# CHAPTER 2
## PLANNING THE TRIP

His eyes snapped open at 0450 (all times herein are in 24-hour format), ten minutes before the alarm was set to ring. Mac sat up, reached over, and switched the alarm off, which was his normal morning routine. He rarely slept until the alarm sounded. Although for the greater part of his adult life Mac had owned his own single-family home, he currently was living in a condo on a golf course in Nebraska. His last posting by the Federal Government had brought him west, and it suited him pretty well despite his deep ties to New England and the ocean.

In addition to his Maine outdoor activities, he had also become a seasoned ocean fisherman. Several years were spent on Cape Cod, Massachusetts, after his divorce in 2003. Mac relocated to the Cape to fish with one of his oldest buddies, Paul. Paul and Mac grew up together in mid-Massachusetts and spent the majority of their early years in the woods or on the water together. They gained some local notoriety as accomplished fishermen at an early age. Both men enlisted in the military, Paul a couple of years ahead of Mac shortly after high school. Paul was deployed to Vietnam and served primarily as a machine gunner carrying the revered M-60, belt-fed, thirty caliber killing machine. He returned as a true hero and was highly decorated for his actions in Southeast Asia. The stories about Paul's war activities are so many and so interesting that it would take a separate writing to even attempt to properly address them. When Mac divorced, his old buddy reached out and invited him to come to the Cape and fish with him on his boat. It was an easy choice, and Mac spent several years learning with Paul, who made fishing an art form. They concentrated on harvesting striped bass and tuna. Paul, incidentally, had taken over 200 giants (fish over six feet) bluefin tuna by himself. He was the source of local legends among Cape fishermen. Mac became a competent fisherman under Paul's tutelage but never aspired or gained the skill and fame that his buddy Paul came by so naturally.

Mac threw on some sweats and eased into the kitchen for his ritual morning cup of coffee. After the coffee, he hit the floor for an hour of push-ups, sit-ups, and a few other exercises. His warm weather routine had become up at 0500, coffee and exercise for about an hour, off to the first tee (he was living on a golf course) and walking the front nine holes. Mac had become a fair golfer and, over the years, thoroughly enjoyed the game that you play against yourself and no one else. Following his front nine, he generally hit the pool for a quick swim, then grabbed breakfast back at his condo. After breakfast, it was back to the course to meet his golf pal, Phil, for the back nine (Phil often joined for the front as well). The two men had become good friends, and Mac enjoyed the game and the comradery. Following the back nine, he would hit the pool again and head home to shower and head for the gym of the gun range. He alternated days for both activities. Still an avid shooter, Mac was set up in his home to make his own bullets. It was a hobby that he enjoyed, and it kept the cost of sending a couple of hundred rounds a week downrange to a reasonable level.

Today, however, Mac sat down with paper and pen to develop a plan for a month-long trip to his beloved lake. Allagash Lake is the holy grail of fishing for the hardiest of Maine fishermen. In the early days, the only access was by canoe, and it was as tough going in (downstream) as coming out (dragging the canoe upstream). In those days, even at ice out when the fishing was at its absolute best, a guy might encounter one or two other anglers and often none during a weeklong trip. Today, however, ice out means big crowds, as many as four or five other groups of one to four men (and even women these days). Mac decided that, in the interest of solitude, he would skip ice out and opt to arrive toward the end of May instead. By the end of May, the lake would be either empty or nearly empty, or things would more closely resemble the early days that Mac so desperately wanted to revisit. There was an issue to contend with as the weather warmed, and that was the Maine State Bird, the blackfly! When the blackflies emerged in the spring, only the most ardent sportsmen considered spending any length of time in the woods. These little pests come in clouds so thick that a man can swipe the air with his hand, close it, and see blood from crushed flies. That's not an embellishment. It's the truth. Often, in the evening, the squadrons of blackflies are accompanied by their dive bomber cousins, mosquitoes, and horseflies. It's said that the horse or deer flies arrive with a knife and fork because they bite so viciously. Mac's old mentors used to say that God blessed northern Maine with bugs because if it weren't for them, the place would be overrun with humans.

Although access to the lake, even today, is very restricted (no closer than a mile at the nearest dirt road), in the early seventies, it was a lot tougher, and the number of hard-core fishermen who made the trip was much lower. Most either knew each other or, at least, had an acquaintance in common. Mac decided to approach the lake the way he did back in the day. There is a logging road that connects with upper Allagash stream about four miles northwest of the lake. He decided to put in there and make the four-mile trip, which in late spring should have enough water to paddle most of the way. The problem is that the canoe must be poled and dragged upstream to return to the launch site at the end of the trip. In years gone by, Mac always had a buddy to help with that chore, but this trip would be a solo event.

The approach and duration of the trip having been decided, the next step was to consider gear for a thirty-day outing. Durability, weight, and reliability were the three most important considerations. For transportation, Mac would be driving his Chevy Silverado 1500 with a tight tonneau cover over the six-foot bed. On the water, he would use his Eagle 16, Class Five Kevlar Canoe. At only sixty-five pounds, it was much lighter than the canoes he had manhandled in the past, and it was nearly indestructible. The next consideration was 'hard gear': necessary equipment that was light enough to haul in and out. He decided to bring a well-stocked first aid kit; a geodesic, two-person dome tent (with fly). A lightweight cot (not critical, but his old bones will be grateful), an ultra-lightweight mummy sleeping bag (rated to zero degrees), a lightweight, military entrenching tool for digging (the earth was cool enough at this time of year to make a great cooler for perishable food), a folding saw, a small axe, parachute cord, cigarette lighters (five), fire starter (flint & steel), knives and compass (at least two), a high-end GPS unit and his new Mossberg backpack 12 gauge with a dozen rounds of slugs (last-ditch defense for unsociable bears), and, of course, a good fly rod and accessories as well as an ultralight spinning rig and some select lures and streamers. Cooking gear would consist of a lightweight grill (foldable tool to rest cooking equipment like the coffee pot on), a coffee pot, a lightweight boiling pot, a small lightweight frying pan, a metal plate and cup, camp fork and spoon, and a lot of tinfoil (most cooking would be done in this lightweight utility).

Clothing is the most critical and often the heaviest gear. In the spring in northern Maine, the temperatures can range from stifling hot to freezing, and it can change faster than you can imagine. Therefore, a guy has to be prepared for anything. Rain is a given, and it can be extended and cold as hell. Being wet for days at forty degrees is a death sentence. In the old days, it was easy. Wool, wool, and wool were the answer. Wool keeps you relatively warm even when wet, and it can be removed as the temperature warms up. The problem is that it's also heavy and bulky. So, at seventy years young, Mac decided that, in addition to his traditional wool toque (slang for wool beanie), gloves, jacket, shirt, pants, socks, and long johns, he would pack a lightweight, down coat and a modern set of rain gear from Cabela's. Wet feet can be a miserable situation, and Mac was certain to get wet, so he planned to pack the following footgear: a lightweight pair of Merrell hiking boots (for nice weather) and another lightweight pair of waterproof (lined) warmer boots and, finally, his lightweight hip waders (bulky but simply wonderful addition to the comfy foot concept)! Last but definitely not least was bug defense gear! At this time of year, you can count on being savagely attacked by black flies and mosquitoes (day and night)! Cold weather is a blessing because you can slap on the wool and be completely comfortable, but when it warms up, you're at their mercy. Therefore, Mac would pack a couple of head nets and several bottles of today's best 'fly dope'!

Food and water are the final considerations. Since Mac planned to make this a lengthy stay food will prove to be a bulky and heavy part of the supplies. No Maine trapper or guide ever goes without some potatoes, onions, salt & pepper, coffee and tea, flour, and, if you really spoil yourself, some butter. Bread (biscuits) will be made from scratch at camp, and fish will be provided.

The campsite Mac selected, although in the old days, it wasn't an approved campsite, will be Sandy Point, which is located not far from the mouth of the access stream at the north end of the lake. Before the white man ever set eyes on this beautiful lake, the Indians used to make camp on these exposed points during warm months. The exposed points served as easy access to the fishing, but, more importantly, they generally had a steady breeze that cut down the horror of the black flies, mosquitoes, and deer flies. The same logic applies today, and that is where Mac will pitch his tent and make camp.

With his plan laid out, Mac set about the task of putting all his gear together, checking the bulk and weight to be sure that the canoe would safely handle the load. Satisfied that his gear was ready, he relocated out to his porch to enjoy an evening coffee and dream about revisiting an old friend, as he always considered the wilderness.

# CHAPTER 3
## TRAVEL TO THE LAKE

It was an 1,800-mile ride from Mac's home in Nebraska to Ashland, Maine, which is the gateway to the Northern Maine Woods and 80 miles from the boat launch on Upper Allagash Stream. Mac decided to take it easy and break the ride into four manageable days of driving. At the gate to the big woods, he would need to check in with the ranger and pay a road usage fee. The fee is a nominal contribution to gain access to the thousands of miles of well-maintained private logging roads in the great North Maine Woods. He would also need to disclose his destination and the expected duration of his trip. To be sure, the ranger will do a second take at a seventy-year-old guy headed into Allagash Lake by canoe and alone for a month. More than likely, Mac and the gate ranger will discuss the old days and some mutually known names of old wardens, guides, and trappers. It won't take very long for the ranger to get the idea that Mac is certainly no stranger to the Maine Wilderness.

The four-day ride was uneventful, and a lot of time was spent remembering the men and the adventures of days gone by. Maylon was Mac's trapping partner, and he was the kind of man that legends are developed about. The Buzzard, as Maylon was known in the outdoors community, was probably the best mink trapper in northern Maine. In the seventies, when Mac was learning the art of mink trapping from

Buzzard, sets were often made where brooks and streams ran under dirt roads. It made for easy access while running long lines (fifty to 100 traps). One day, as they approached a favorite set, Mac noticed that another trapper had already set the spot. "We better move on," Mac said to Buzzard, who just turned and said, "Why would we do that. We'll just mosey up the brook a way and catch them before they ever get to the road." That's exactly what they did, too. Buzzard would stand and stare at a brook, take a deep draw on his unfiltered cigarette, and read the sign. He could, inevitably, make a set that would produce. It wasn't magic or luck that gave him his edge. It was years of living in the woods with the animals. He had come to understand and respect them. You might ask how someone who claimed to understand, respect, and love the animals could undertake such a cruel activity as trapping them. The answer is complex. You would have to have lived in that time and place to even begin to understand it. Buzzard would sooner injure a man long before a wild animal, and his sets were always as humane as possible. Our mink sets were always drowning sets. The trap was attached to a wire line that followed into deep water, where the animal would wind up quickly and die fast. It sounds horrible but, like I said, you would have to have lived it.

When Mac (Lizard, as Buzzard referred to him) and Buzzard first started trapping together, Mac had a tendency to talk too much. After several scoldings by his mentor, Mac began to ease up on the chatter. One evening at Lower Ellis Pond (not far from Allagash Lake), the two men spent an entire afternoon fishing and then made dinner without uttering a single word. After dinner, Buzzard, sitting by the fire, took a snap from his bottle of bourbon and said, "That was a great conversation, Lizard."

Mac was confused and said, "What conversation?"

"Exactly," muttered the older outdoorsman and actually forced a smile of sorts. That was the backwoods that Mac yearned so desperately for.

Mac finally arrived at the Ashland check station, "Gateway to The North Maine Woods." The check station is about six miles into the woods from Ashland after just crossing the upper end of the Aroostook River. Mac wheeled his Chevy to the right and parked just outside the station. The station itself was a small one-room wood shack equipped with an old desk and, of course, a wood stove. The walls were pasted with pictures of sports at their camps and posing with trophy fish and other game. Mac eyed an old picture that really struck a heavy chord in his heart. It was from 1972 and pictured Mac and the Buzzard squatted by a campfire at Second Musquacook Lake at a spot known to old guides as The Squirrel Pocket. In those days, a man could stand on the shore and catch five-pound lake trout all day in the early spring. Good times!

The attendant must have noticed Mac fixated on the picture and asked, "Someone you recognize?" Mac turned, and before he could answer, the attendant spouted, "Jesus fucking Christ, you're Buzzard's mink-trapping partner!"

"Guilty as charged," Mac shot back. "I'm sorry, I don't seem to remember you."

The man, probably in his forties, said, "I was just a kid when you guys were doing your thing. I met you a few times with my GrandPaw John."

"You mean John, the warden supervisor?" Mac queried.

"Yup, he used to bust your balls, but he really liked you guys. I guess he respected the way you did things." A compliment from that man was one of the greatest honors a trapper or guide could ever hope to receive.

He was a genuine legend in the North Maine Woods. Once, Mac and CK, another of his early-day mentors, were on a four-day fishing trip out near Spider Lake. They were in for summer brookies (brook trout or square tails, as you prefer). In those days, a brookie had to be at least six inches to keep. The idea was to maintain enough small fish to resupply the resource for future sports. The two men had pulled over by a brook that ran down towards the Realty Road from the north, and they knew that there were no legal-size fish there to speak of. A truck was parked on the side of the road, and they knew damn well that the man or men who were fishing the brook weren't legal. CK was just finishing his non-filtered Pall Mall when a warden truck rolled up and stopped. It was a Sunday morning, and the woods were, other than this parking lot, quiet. John stepped out of his truck and walked toward CK and Mac. John was a tall, lean man with broad shoulders and eyes that drilled holes into you. "I guess you're not fishing the brook?" he asked.

"Nope," CK snapped back, "but somebody is."

"Ayuh," John answered. "No legal fish 'upta that beaver pond, ya' know."

"Ayuh, that's my take," CK agreed.

"Well, might as well get to it," John announced as he stepped right into the brook and started upstream. He was walking in the brook because the alders along the side made walking almost impossible.

CK said, "Wanna' hang around for the show?"

Mac figured it would take a half hour to reach the dam, maybe another half hour to make the arrest, and thirty more minutes to walk them out. "Sure, this gotta be good," Mac said. "I reckon that a couple of beers might not do much harm." CK agreed and the two guys grabbed a beer each from one of the well-stocked coolers and copped a squat in the shade.

Almost two hours passed before the men heard the first splashes in the brook. "Must be getting' close," CK volunteered.

"Ayuh, I can hear them bitching right now." Mac was laughing already. Finally, two men and a living legend appeared some thirty yards upstream. The men were each carrying two five-gallon pails and their fishing gear. They were sweating like pigs and breathing hard, but John looked like nothing had happened except for his wet pants.

They all paraded over to John's vehicle, and he spread out some plastic bags on the ground. "Pour 'em out and count 'em," he ordered.

They had taken more than fifty small trout, and each one earned them a hefty fine as well as the loss of their fishing licenses. John could have impounded their truck, but then he'd have to endure their presence even longer. The paperwork was completed, and the two men were released with a pending court date. John turned to CK after the other two were gone and said, "Cold ones, eh?" In those days, even though driving and drinking was illegal, a beer or two that far back in, provided you weren't being an idiot, was just not considered an issue.

"Want one?" CK said, offering the warden a frosty cold Bud. He never said yes but accepted the beer and sat down to enjoy it. Those were the days, and that was the kind of man that John was (regular as mud, but all business with no frills).

"That's the Squirrel Pocket in the picture, isn't it?" the attendant pressed.

"Ahuh, that's where we were."

"Who took the picture?" he continued to press for information.

"You see that stringer of fish?" Mac asked.

"Yup..." was the response.

"Well, that's a little over the limit, don't you guess? So, it's probably just as well that we don't go there... okay?" Mac posed.

"I bet I know who it was, considering where you were and when?" the attendant continued. "Maybe," was all Mac had to say on the matter.

"Where 'ya headed, Mac?" It was a required question for all sports headed into the North Maine Woods through a check station.

"Headed to Allagash Lake, putting in on the upper branch at the landing. I'll be in for about a month," Mac politely answered.

"Alone? That's a rough haul alone, and you're..." he stopped short of calling Mac old.

"I'm not in a hurry, and it's not my first trip back in, son." Mac's answer was courteous but definitive. He was alone and that was the way he wanted it.

"Okay, Mac."

Mac paid the entry fee, said so long to the younger man, and disappeared in a cloud of dust. The dry roads always raised a dust storm behind a moving truck.

It was May 28, the sky was bright blue, and the sun was warm as Mac headed southwest for his nearly 100-mile dirt road excursion to Allagash Lake. Mac planned to wander out to John's Bridge, which was one of the only places to cross the Allagash Wilderness Waterway, then on to the Upper Allagash Landing, where he would finally put into Allagash Stream. He was looking at close to five hours of cruising the same logging roads that he and Buzzard had driven almost fifty years earlier. As long as you aren't behind another vehicle (especially a logging truck), you can run with your windows down and enjoy the smells of the wilderness coming back to life. It's a magic place and for a man who has lived intimately with the backcountry, the memories never seem to fade away.

Drinking directly from open water is frowned upon these days, but Mac had lived his entire life doing just that. The water from a spring running down to a brook or stream is the most delicious thirst quencher in the world. He eased the Chevy off to the side of the road at a spring that he remembered from his trapping days. As he dismounted the vehicle to fill his thermos, he heard the first 'peepers' for the trip. Peepers are small frogs that are gray, tan, or light brown in color with a light belly. They can be identified by the dark "X" on their backs and bands on their legs. The toes have flat pads that secrete mucous, which acts as an adhesive to aid in climbing. An adult is between ¾ – 1 ¼ inches in length. Their song or peeping is unmistakable and has always had a soul-soothing effect on Mac. It's funny, he thought, how sounds and smells can awaken memories from the past. Some are wonderful, and some are horrible, but they can be recalled just the same. For Mac, the peepers have always been a therapeutic song.

Mac sat in his truck and had a long draw on his thermos. The cold, sweet water, and the sound of the peepers just off the road were just the catalyst he needed to drift off into peaceful thought. "Why can't society be more like nature?" he wondered. Out here things are what they are simply because that's the way it is. No need to rationalize or justify why a coyote kills a mouse or even a deer to feed itself. There is no call to question the motive of a breeding pair of loons. They will mate for life, as do the Canada Geese, while a buck deer will tend to as many as he can during the rut (mating season). There is no judgment as to which is more correct; it simply is the way it is, and it works. "Seems like people could, and should, slow down and stop overthinking everything. Maybe it's that brain of ours that's causing so much trouble. Some things just need to be accepted, especially things that are in step with nature," he mused as he fired up the Chevy and hit the road again.

It was about 1400 (02:00 PM) when he crossed John's Bridge and closed the gap to the landing in a little over an hour. He stopped and got out to just watch the river flowing north, as it had done for centuries. There was no other traffic, and the sound and smell of the spring-high water again flooded his mind with memories of the many canoe trips that he had guided down the Allagash back in the seventies.

One trip in particular stood out. It was 1975, and he was making the Allagash run with an Air Force buddy named Denny. Denny was a rugged New Hampshire man, but he had never spent any serious time in the deep backwoods. They were in an eighteen-foot Old Town canoe, and as they entered Round Pond (one of several larger bodies of water that were part of the Allagash Wilderness Waterway), Mac ran the canoe to the right and along the edge of the pond. He was having a look to see if there were any fiddleheads (the furled fronds of a young fern that are harvested as a vegetable). As he paddled (no motors were allowed on the Allagash), he approached a huge hemlock tree with a branch that extended about fifteen feet out over the water. A movement from above caught Mac's eye, and what he saw when he looked up at the overhanging branch took his breath away. It was the long tail of a big cat (eastern cougar) hanging down. Mac started to ease the canoe back into deeper water and softly told Denny to look at the branch. Just about the time that Denny's eyes fixed on the animal the cat let go a roar that made both their skins crawl. Denny let out a scream of his own, and Mac never figured out who was more frightened, Denny or the big cat. Sightings like that were rare and Mac had been fortunate enough to have had several over his tenure in the woods. Mountain lions were once common in Maine but, since the turn of the last century, became increasingly scarce and were not considered to exist in Maine at all. Evidently, a few cats never got the message, though.

Mac snapped back to the present, hopped into his truck, and pressed on, still physically laughing at the memory of his buddy's reaction that day. He made the landing around 1530 and decided to make an overnight camp right there and hit the water in the morning. It was warm and dry, so he decided to sleep under the stars by his campfire. Some beans and brown bread for supper and a good cup of coffee and the tired old woodsman drifted off to sleep as content as a man has the right to be.

# CHAPTER 4
## DOWN THE STREAM

Mac crawled out of his sleeping back at around 0500, and the woods were just coming to life. It was a cool, dry day, and after his morning relief, Mac just sat on a rock by the stream to watch and listen to the world waking up as he had done so many times before. First, the birds begin to chatter (even before sunrise). The other daytime critters begin moving around while the nocturnal animals are heading to cover.

The landing was located by a nice pool in the stream, probably four feet deep and maybe fifty yards across. As the sun poked out, Mac heard a splash, and his eyes were immediately drawn to the ripples left from a brookie snagging a fly for breakfast. In the distance, he heard a loon call out. The sound of a loon wailing is very distinct. The wail is most commonly used for long-distance communication between mated pairs of loons. Loon pairs may also wail to one another as they begin to engage with an intruding loon. During periods of high stress, such as when encountering a perceived threat to its nest or chicks, a loon may give a more frantic-sounding wail. In these situations, the wail will typically have three or more syllables and may be interspersed with other calls that denote stress, such as the tremolo or the yodel. The wail is frequently heard during night chorusing.

The old woodsman measured the value of the peace and organization he had come to treasure in the deep woods. "You can't buy this with money," he mused. A business partner once spouted that he owned Mac, and Mac responded that no one could own another man and that all his money could never buy the true wealth that is available at no cost in nature. The shame of it is that only those lucky few ever get to really understand that. "Too bad that society, as we know it, can't seem to function with the magnificent order and calm that exists in the wild. In the wild, there can be moments of violence (predators taking food and the like), but it all occurs with this wonderful sense of fulfillment of a greater plan, and there is no deliberate infliction of harm in acquiring individual wealth or prosperity. It's just a cycle that works and has worked flawlessly since the dawn of time."

A quick breakfast of black coffee (always tastes so much better by an open fire), some bacon & beans with a chunk of brown bread, and it was time to hit the water. Mac eased the canoe into the stream and carefully arranged the load, accounting for weight disbursement and protection from water. It was about four miles (considering all the bends in the stream) to the lake and on foot, which would take about three hours or so, but by water, it would depend entirely on how many beaver ponds he had to portage. The beaver has always been active on the stream, and sometimes they make travel easier, but some dams require either a tough drag over the damn or a portage around it on land. It's all part of the game, though.

It was a beautiful morning, warm for the season (around forty-five degrees at daybreak), and a light breeze from the northwest even made things better.

*Maybe I should orient you, dear reader:*

*Allagash Lake is basically a north/south body of water with two approaches. A walk-in to the south from the Allagash Lake Gate and the water route from Allagash Lake Landing via the stream on the north. The stream approaches from the northwest and meets the lake at the northwest corner near Ledge Point. Therefore, a northwest (or following wind) makes paddling that much easier.*

The canoe eased into the stream, and Mac started downstream, seeming to fall deeper into a world of memories with each stroke. The stream runs around two to three feet deep on average in the spring, making canoe travel pleasant. This spring, everything was perfect, and as the sun rose higher in the east, the day warmed. The metamorphosis from barren to lush green is dramatic in the Maine springtime backcountry. Today, the trees, although not fully leafed, had a hue of green and red (buds) that softened the harsh winter landscape remarkably. The air was clean, and the 'spring smell' was intoxicating. You could feel the world embracing the change of season. Mating was everywhere, and all seemed in balance with nature. Mac couldn't help comparing this peace and tranquility to the turmoil that the world was experiencing. For all the violence and apparent cruelty in the wilderness, there is an overarching calm and sense of order. It just all makes sense. He thought about humans as a species. There seemed to be a few interesting facts that aren't often addressed anymore. For example, in all of recorded history and in tales passed down by story before the written word existed, nearly every society globally has looked to a higher power. Maybe it's an inherent need to rationalize but maybe, just maybe, there is more to it. When you're alone in the wilderness, the order, the beauty, the symbiotic relationships (harsh and otherwise) pop out at you, and you can't help thinking that it's more than chance that perfected it all. Sure, it could all have happened by chance, but the perfection of it all makes a person take a hard second look. In the order of things, mating (procreation) can't be overlooked, and that speaks directly to the current mess we find ourselves in with respect to gender identification and sex discrimination. Animals (and we are animals) predominately mate as males and females. It's not too tough to figure out why. Males, across the board, are larger, although not always more dominant, but they are physically different from females. It's simple genetics, for the most part. Mac mused on the concept of gender equality. He figured that there is no question that in our species, men and women are different (same throughout the animal kingdom), and that doesn't mean that females are inferior to males. It just means that they are different. *For example, dear reader,* any woodsman (and that is intended to include both genders) knows that messing with a mama bear with cubs or a cow moose with a calf or two is infinitely more dangerous than screwing with a male of either species. Both species produce larger males, but these females are strong and formidable creatures. The same principle applies to humans. Although males are generally larger framed, Mac had seen female soldiers (who could have won a swimsuit competition) drag a 200-pound man by the neck out of harm's way in a battle. So, why do we have to constantly fight amongst ourselves and argue for superiority? Why can't we appreciate the physical difference and focus on mutual respect and acceptance of the 'way things are'?

The intensifying squeal of a nested osprey broke the daydream and snapped Mac back to reality. "Christ, she's beautiful," he thought as he drifted some forty feet below her nest, which was constructed near the top of a dead maple alongside the stream. The rest of the morning was a series of pleasantries and a very easy paddle. He made the final right bend around 1030 AM, and the lake slipped into view. He drew a deep breath and just drifted the last few hundred feet, bathed in the morning sun and feeling his soul coming to one with this paradise on earth.

# CHAPTER 5
## THE CAMPSITE

Mac eased his canoe onto the gentle sandy shore at Sandy Point Campsite, located right at the mouth of the stream on the northwest corner of the lake. In the old days, this was just a sandy beach with no amenities, but today, the Maine Forestry Service, in an effort to protect the environment and to make camping more pleasant for visitors, has improved the site to contain pre-built fireplaces and even an outhouse (like being in the city ... LOL). One disadvantage is that years ago, deadwood was readily available for campfires, but today, you need to wander deeper into the woods to gather firewood (not a big deal, though). Mac carried a lightweight bow saw that did the job nicely.

It was a beautiful morning. There was a light southwest breeze, and only a few puffy clouds dotted the sky. Mac sat on a rock facing southeast, which presented most of the lake with the fire tower hill on the western shore.

Almost due south of Mac's campsite is another interesting spot called the ice caves. They are a series of fissure caves located nearly at the top of a significant hill. The caves are tight, cold, and wet so most casual explorers only venture in 50 to 100 feet. They extend into a vast network, but it's mostly left alone. *A point of interest dear reader,* the caves are full of rather pale-colored and fairly docile spiders.

There isn't much written about them, but Mac remembered his first and rather unpleasant encounter years ago. He was just a young pup in those days, and on his first trip into the lake with old Buzzard, he insisted on going in to have a look. Buzzard fired up a smoke and said, "Knock 'yerself out, Lizard... you ain't gonna be in there very long." He sort of giggled to himself, and Mac recalled wondering what horrible detail he was deliberately omitting. Not being fond of tight places in the first place, Mac reluctantly crawled into the cave. He had a small flashlight and was only wearing a T-shirt because it was very warm outside. Only about twenty feet into the black hole, he felt what he thought was moss or roots on his neck and arms. He instinctively reached back to brush the debris from his neck, but the damn thing was crawling right down his arm. He then realized that he had probably a half dozen spiders crawling on him. "Jesus fucking Christ," he said out loud. He was completely freaked out and backpedaled out as fast as he could. As he broke back into the sunlight, he could hear old Buzzard belly laughing. "Didn't figure you'd last very long in there, Lizard," Mayland barked. Mac was actually shivering as he frantically stripped naked in an attempt to rid himself of the grotesque arachnids. "Now that's what I call a funny sight," Buzzard noted out loud. Mac didn't share the humor.

The evening wasn't far off, and the campsite was pretty much established, so Mac decided to hit the water to snag a couple of fish for supper. It was a really beautiful evening with a light southwest breeze and a cloudless sky. As he eased the now empty canoe into the crystal-clear water, Mac felt a welcome sense of calm and order. It brought him back to simpler times as a younger man. He had always found refuge in the wilderness, and this was exactly the therapy he sought to put his mind in balance once again.

A loon seemed to greet him, singing out their crazy call. It was a welcome addition to this God-given therapy. Then, a surface splash not far from the shore caught his attention. From the ripple in the water, he guessed that some brookies were availing themselves of a new hatch (insect larvae emerging from the water) for their dinner. He tied on one of Buzzard's go-to flies, a muddler minnow (brown deer hair fly), and gently presented it to the surface near the last roll (fish swallowing a surface insect). It no sooner settled on the water than a nice brookie sucked in down. He harvested three trout that averaged around a pound and headed back in to prepare his own supper.

It had been a great day. Mac sat by his little campfire, his belly full, enjoying a nice evening tea and the changing sounds that now included the lapping of water on the sandy shore, the loon's mystical orchestra, and the first evening cries of a pack of coyotes that were not too far away. To someone not fully comfortable with being alone in the wilderness, these sounds might be disturbing, but to Mac, they were the sounds of everything being in perfect balance, and that, *dear reader*, was exactly why he was here in the first place.

As the last light faded, Mac crawled into his sleeping bag and drifted off to a beautiful and restful sleep. The upheaval being experienced around the globe had been washed away by nature's perfect order and simplicity.

# CHAPTER 6
## THE ADVENTURE BEGINS

"A pressure from within me has torn me from my rest, as dormant senses spring to life, the sun begins to crest..." These words from a poem he penned a long time ago came to mind as Mac crawled out of the tent to greet the new day. It was a cool morning with almost no wind and a magnificent sunrise. As Mac got the morning fire going, he was bathed in the serenity of this wonderful place. An eagle circling above let out its distinctive scream, and he watched a pair of otters playing no more than thirty yards offshore. Hot, black coffee and a few pieces of jerky that he'd packed in provided the kickstart he sought. He was on the lake to fish and relax, and the latter took precedence for this morning. Mac sat for a long time just soaking in the dawning day and decided to take a paddle along the shore, just because. There was another campsite on the north shore only a half mile west of his camp, so Mac cruised along the shoreline to check out the other site.

At about 0830, it happened. Mac saw a sort of light flash that was different from anything he had ever experienced and at the same time, felt a very subtle wave of air, but there was no wing and no disturbance of the calm lake water. Strange, he thought and then just dismissed the event from his mind. Rounding the bend in the shoreline, Mac saw smoke rising from the other side and figured he had company on the lake. Sure enough, as the campsite came into view, Mac saw a tent and a canoe. When he was just off the landing, he shouted, "Hello in, Camp" (a common greeting used when approaching the camp of someone unknown to him). His call was not answered, so Mac beached his canoe and cautiously approached the tent. He noted fishing and cooking gear, and the site seemed like your typical fishing getaway. *Perhaps the guy is just shore fishing,* he thought. It was unusual but not unheard of for one or two guys to be out here, and like him, they probably didn't anticipate company.

A snapped twig caught Mac's ear, and he instinctively swung toward the sound. He chuckled to himself, thinking, "You're on Allagash Lake, not in a combat zone." Clearly, someone or something was moving through the brush toward the campsite. A moment later, a single guy broke into the open campsite. He was a slightly framed dude around 5'7" wearing typical backwoods attire and a boonie hat.

"I called out before coming in," Mac said.

"I heard you," came the reply, but the voice startled old Mac. It sounded feminine and then Mac received a real surprise. The slightly framed dude was, in fact, a girl. She ditched the boonie hat, revealing a close-cropped but very feminine mess of beautiful black hair and the most riveting blue eyes Mac had ever seen. When she shed her fishing vest it revealed a gorgeous frame, lean and solid. "Yep, I'm a girl... surprised?" she said.

Mac was completely caught off guard, and sort of stumbled through his answer like a lovestruck schoolboy. "Well, it isn't every day that you bump into a lady out here," he said.

"My Mom is a lady. Why don't you call me Danie," she quipped. "Daniel, if it makes you more comfortable."

"I'm Mac, Charlie McNamara."

"Well, hi, Mac," she responded. "I didn't notice any other camps on my way in," she offered.

"I'm camped up on the north shore. I canoed down the upper branch."

"Okay, that explains it. I portaged to the south end and worked my way up here along the north shoreline." Most canoers kept pretty close to the shore as much as possible since winds can come up out of nowhere and the tranquil lake can become treacherous. "When did you arrive?" Mac asked.

"I just made camp this afternoon. I was getting rid of breakfast in the bushes when I heard you call out."

"You're alone?" Mac pressed.

"Yep, I really love this place and my own company," she shot back.

"Do any fishing yet?" Mac asked her.

"Nope, but I was planning on wetting a fly around sunset. If you're not some psychopath, maybe we can hit it together," she said with a chuckle.

"Well, I don't reckon that I'm dangerous, and two paddling is always better, provided you can put the fly on the water and not in my ear," Mac responded. The ice was now broken, and since it was still early in the day, Mac suggested that they run up to his camp for some lunch and to catch the brookies that lay in the cooler water from the stream.

"Sounds like a plan," Danie said, and she began to put together the gear she needed for the evening fishing.

"Let's take my boat. Two paddling makes easy travel. I'll run you back to your site before dark." It was agreed, and while they covered the half-mile ride, Mac continued to inquire about his new friend. It turned out that Danie was a geologist and an anthropologist as well. Besides fishing, she was interested in the ice caves. As they talked, she revealed a pretty incredible knowledge of the early Indians who lived in the area and believed they may have used the ice caves to store meat and fish. The temperature inside the cave's hoovers was around forty degrees all year, which made it a natural refrigerator.

When they arrived at Mac's camp, Danie noticed two lawn chairs by the fireplace. "Expecting company?" she asked with a beautiful smile.

"I found out a long time ago that an extra chair in camp is never a bad idea," Mac replied. He rustled up some leftover beans and potatoes, and they sat together, eating, and sucking up the serenity. It was a leisurely afternoon, and somehow, the conversation drifted into current affairs. Mac offered his not-so-humble opinion about the current state of the country. He told her that a big part of why he had returned to this place was to regain a sense of perspective. He explained that in his younger days, his backwoods travels were always the most relaxing and rewarding. He told her his thoughts about the simplicity and synergy that existed in the wild and how he wondered why people seemed to have lost their connection to the wilderness.

"Seems like there's more to you than broad shoulders, bud," she said. She went on to explain that she also felt like everything was in balance in the wild and that, having studied Indigenous peoples from around the world, she believed that the further removed from nature a society becomes, the more they become susceptible to greed and perversion. Mac couldn't have agreed more, not to mention that he'd become completely smitten by the beautiful, intelligent girl.

"See that... trout are beginning to rise. Let's go catch some dinner." Danie agreed, and they slid the canoe into the pristine water. They fished for about an hour and released all the trout after the first five or six. It was coming on dark, and a beautiful moon had edged its way into the evening sky. They arrived back at Danie's camp just after dark and she asked Mac if he'd be okay going back at night. He assured her this was where he was at his best, and after getting her gear stowed, he just said goodnight and started to shove off.

"Let's have breakfast together in the morning," she asked.

"Okay, I'll swing by at daybreak." With that, he paddled out onto the lake. He had a light following wind, so the ride would be pleasant. *Holy shit*, he thought as he glided across the moonlit lake. *What's happening here? I came out to be alone and get a reboot and find myself in the company of the most beautiful, smart, and funny girl I've ever met,* he thought. The ride took twice as long as it should have because Mac just drifted a lot, listening to the loons and the other nighttime sounds. Keeping the shoreline in sight, he finally arrived at his camp. He stowed his gear and lit a fire. He could see the reddish glow from Danie's fire a half mile away. He wasn't hungry but he made some tea, and while the kettle heated, he stripped down and took a swim in the cool waters. It was cool enough to keep the mosquitoes and black flies down, and as he sat and sipped his tea, his mind reeled. *This just can't be happening*, he thought. I*t's too perfect and almost possible.* Finally, he became drowsy and crawled into his sleeping bag. He set his wind-up alarm for an hour before daylight and drifted off into a remarkable sleep.

A massive clap of thunder snapped Mac from his deep sleep. It was already 0330 and there was a corker of a thunderstorm raging. The wind was hard out of the southwest and he was grateful he packed a geodesic 4-man tent. These tents are popular in Alaska due to their wind and precipitation protection. His first thought was Danie's very basic little pup tent. *She must be getting pounded*, he thought. There wasn't anything he could do but wait for daylight to assess the situation.

As daylight began to take shape, the storm seemed to have no letup. Mac knew that a canoe on that water was extremely dangerous, so he decided to throw on his rain gear and make his way to Danie's campsite on foot. It was only about a half mile, so he set off.

About forty-five minutes after he started walking, he came in sight of her campsite. The wind and rain had gotten even worse, and it was driving straight into her little tent. "Hello in, Camp," he shouted, and this time she answered.

"What the hell are you doing out in this shit?" she responded. He poked his head into her tent and saw it was drenched, and she was in full rain gear.

"Nice morning... eh," he shot back with a broad smile. "You look really comfortable." Danie just stared at him in amazement. "I have much better conditions at my camp. How about hiking back with me to get dry and have breakfast?"

"Sounds good to me," she answered.

She didn't need much more than she was wearing, so the two headed back to Mac's camp. When they arrived, Mac suggested she go inside and get comfortable while he got a fire going. He had set up a tarp for shelter by his fire, so despite the horrible conditions, he was pretty comfortable. He had a supply of dry wood and kindling stowed under another small tarp, and the smell of fresh coffee soon worked its way through the wind to her nose. She came out, and they sat in the two chairs and downed a few cups of coffee and had potatoes and fresh trout for breakfast.

"Looks like we have a lot of time to kill, so how about telling me about you," Mac queried.

"Okay, but let's start with you first." Her smile was mesmerizing, and Mac agreed. He began with his youth. He'd always been a hunter/fisher and developed a deep connection with the wild early on. He explained that he was stationed in northern Maine as an air traffic controller where he met his mentors like CK and Buzzard. He explained that they took him under their wing and passed years of wilderness experience (the stuff you can't learn in books). He detailed his first TDY (temporary duty assignment) to Thailand in '71. He was stationed at Nakhon Phanom Royal Thai Air Force Base, where he manned a U.S. FPN47 mobile radar unit. TDY's were only six months long, but during that time, he made some great friends with the Green Berets (Greenies), who ran patrols deep into Laos. The base was only thirty miles from the Ho Chi Minh Trail, which moved like a snake as it suited the VC (Viet Cong). After a month or so he offered to travel with them as a mule, carrying M60 belts and other gear because one of their team had been seriously hurt. That could never happen today, but things were very different forty years ago. He was offered an opportunity to swap over to the Army from the Air Force at the end of his TDY, but being recently married, he declined. He told several stories about air traffic control, including another deployment to England in 1976. He had been assigned a three-year tour (an overseas long) at RAF Bentwaters in Suffolk.

In the spring of 1980 Mac received a request to accept a voluntary assignment that was classified, and no one on his base had a clue where he'd be going or what the job was. Initially, his commanding officer refused to allow the assignment, but no sooner had he refused than orders came down from headquarters dictating that Mac was to deploy. He was immunized for worldwide service and issued everything from artic to jungle gear. He could hardly lug all of it around. His flight stopped in Germany for briefings. When he got off the EAGLE flight, he was met by military police who immediately took all his gear and told him that he would be outfitted with only mission-essential gear. The first meeting was with ununiformed men he could only assume were CIA operatives. There were several other airmen with him, and nobody knew what to expect. At this time, chemical warfare was a front-row matter, and one of the airmen asked about chem suits. The spook running the brief just said if you're attacked, they won't do you any good and proceeded to run a film. It was a Russian training film where they used chemical and blood agents on their own troops. It was the most horrible thing Mac had ever seen or even imagined. Needless to say, that scared the living shit out of everyone. They were told that no form of ID would be carried, and no rank insignia would be worn. There were two other controllers and a few maintenance guys with Mac. Several days of pre-deployment would be conducted in Germany and then wheels up in a C-130 for... well, no one knew except the flight crew. The 130 touched down on a bare-bones runway in a desert, so we all knew that this was in support of Operation Eagle Claw (the Iranian hostage crisis). When the door of the C-130 opened, it was like stepping into an oven. It was around 120 degrees, and the sun was absolutely brutal. The commanding officer was a full colonel, and he laid down the law in plain English. He said that no rank was authorized, and no one was to salute anyone at any time.

Mac got settled and met his ATC crew in short order. He was assigned to manage the FPN-47 (mobile radar unit), and the senior air traffic controller would manage the TSW7 (mobile tower). Clearly, Mac's experience at NKP was why he was selected. Everyone settled into a daily routine, and, for the most part, it was more boring than anything else. That all came to an abrupt end one morning when they were working in a C-140 from Germany with supplies and replacement troops. The weather was perfect (if you like the surface of the sun), but all arriving aircraft were given radar advisories because the heat caused a mirage effect that displaced the runway landing threshold. It's like the waves you see coming off a paved road on a very hot day.

This day, when the C-140 was on about a six-mile final, Mac walked behind the PAR (precision approach radar) controller, who was responsible for azimuth and elevation advisories. Mac almost shit his pants because he immediately recognized that the PAR was improperly aligned. He threw the controller out of the seat and made the correction in record time. At three miles, it was clear that the 140 was too low, and Mac issued a go-around. The pilot, an air National Guard troop with no desert experience, came back saying it was all good and he had the runway. Mac ordered him to make a missed approach, but the order was ignored. In seconds, the 140 began touching down, but it was a good half mile from the runway. Mac hit the tower and radar bailout, and as his team of four controllers piled out of the unit, the jet was detonating anti-tank mines and anti-personnel mines. It was indescribably horrific. The huge jet was exploding and plowing down the runway right toward Mac and his guys. All of his team managed to get out of the way by the skin of their teeth. They had friends on that plane and all hands were tasked with recovering bodies when the heat subsided. So much for boredom!

During the first month on the firebase, Mac made friends with the special forces guys, who all kept to themselves. Like in Thailand, Mac was drawn to those guys. They finally warmed up to Mac because, in their words, he was as batshit crazy as they were. Mac had been begging to go on patrol with them, but it was a dead end. The SF (special forces) team consisted of Navy Seals, ranger regiment boys, and a British SAS officer. Turns out this was the first sanctioned joint special forces operation. The beginning of Delta Force and JAYSOC (Joint Special Forces Command). One evening, the team chief told Mac that one of his guys had gotten very sick and he needed a mule (a guy who hadn't trained with the team to be used to carry ammo and gear). Mac was ecstatic, but although he was qualified on the weapons and radios, he had not trained with the team, so under no conditions was he to engage if the enemy was encountered. That was the word of God!

The team was flown out in a relatively new UH-60 chopper in the evening to the eastern edge of the hills bordering the Red Sea. The idea was a long foot patrol looking for insurgents camped in the hills. The night was eerily bright, with a full moon providing a surreal illumination. The very small six-man team moved out, quietly communicating with each other with the latest throat mic comms.

"We covered about five miles meandering through the rocky terrain, and the chief called for a break. We hydrated, and I was told that this is the way most patrols go—no action, just a job—but I was firmly reminded that in the event of an encounter, I was to take cover and not engage! Well, it wasn't another mile when all hell broke loose! The surreal night was broken by flashes of gunfire, and the deadly quiet was broken by gunfire. Most people, I guess from watching movies, expect full auto fire all the time, but the reality is that, except for suppression fire, most operatives prefer semi-auto, which conserves ammo and improves accuracy. I took cover, as directed, behind some large rocks while the team and the enemy fought it out. For the record, anyone who tells you that they aren't afraid during a firefight is either a liar or a psychopath. The noise is deafening, and your adrenaline goes full throttle. I saw an enemy combatant moving from right to left about sixty meters ahead of me. I knew that I wasn't to engage but couldn't allow him to potentially take out a team member, so I took aim with my M16A1 rifle and dropped him in his tracks. Evidently, my muzzle flash caught the attention of his buddies because bullets started crackling by me, and the sandstone rock that I was taking cover behind began to take hits, lots of hits. I returned fire, but due to a long time out of actual combat, I burned through ammo much too fast. I was, admittedly, overexcited. In no time, I exhausted my ammo, so I moved toward the first dude that I dropped and grabbed his AK47 and his available mags. I no sooner shouldered the enemy weapon than another combatant appeared in the dim light. I opened fire, the weapon was selected to full auto, and he did a back flip, having received several rounds to the chest area. Then everything went dead silent again.

As I knelt by another rock, I felt a firm hand on my shoulder while the rifle I was holding was also held by someone else. I was shit scared, but before I could even move, I heard the chief's gruff voice say, 'Drop the weapon, cherry,' an expression denoting my inexperience with the team." I released my grip on the Avtomat Kalashnikova and turned to the chief. To my amazement, the whole team was right there behind me.

"What part of do not engage did you miss in the mission brief?" he snapped. Then he busted out laughing and said, "Okay, you can hike with us anytime, cherry." The whole incident took only ten or fifteen minutes, and at the end, four enemy combatants were dead, and I had dumped two of them. Now, the adrenaline kicked in, and I began to shake uncontrollably.

"Ya need to conserve ammo, cherry. Other than that, ya did great," another team member chimed in. We finished the patrol and then got picked up and flown back to the firebase where the Jack Daniels and stories flowed freely. Over the next month in the desert, I accompanied the guys on several patrols without incident. When the op ended, and we were all headed back to our home bases, I was asked to consider swapping over from the Air Force to the Navy and also to the Army for special forces training. I had been married just before the deployment and, regretfully, declined both offers, but to this day, I'm not sure it was the right decision."

Mac continued by telling Danie he'd like to make the conversation a two-way event and invited her to share a little more about herself. Danie suddenly morphed from a smiling, apparently happy-hearted gal into a deeper and deadly serious woman. Mac was visibly taken aback as she began to speak. She opened with a somber statement saying, "Mac, I wanted to delay opening up to you until we had more time to get acquainted by, I guess circumstances dictate that it's going to be now rather than later. Please be patient and let me finish before you pass any judgment on my integrity and perhaps my sanity.

"I was born in the year 2246 and I've been tasked with the mission to travel here in an effort to help the United States back to a country that holds integrity, family, moral values, and true freedom as its fundamental structure." Mac began to break in, but she urged him to wait. "In my home, time travel has recently become a reality, and although things a vastly different, we have witnessed the deterioration of the United States and its global implications with horror. Unlike the science fiction stories of your century, the reality is that a traveler cannot return to his or her own time, at least not yet. My volunteering for this task means that I'm locked in this time permanently."

"I'm not sure if I'm terrified or amazed," Mac responded.

"That's a perfectly expected reaction," she explained. "We have time, here alone on this beautiful lake, to talk at length about my mission and why I'm sitting here with you specifically. It's not an accident that we have chosen you as our point of contact. Your entire life so far has been an example of what we consider the foundation for a leader to guide America back to its noble path."

"Hold it," Mac interrupted. "Even if everything that you're saying is true, and I'm definitely not sold on the fact that you're even sane, there is absolutely nothing special about me. I'm just a regular guy and one who's made more than his share of mistakes."

"That's exactly why we selected you, Mac. You have been wise enough to actually learn along the road of life. For example: why are you here today? We know that you became completely frustrated with the direction that things have taken and returned to a place where you often came to embrace the magnificence of nature. Here, you can evaluate the differences as well as the synergy between the natural world and the one created by man. Don't get me wrong, Mac, there are millions of wonderful people in the country, but their voices are increasingly muffled by extremists with high-profile voices that are embraced by corporate-controlled media. The country desperately needs a good man or woman to become the spokesperson for the genuine good population. A person to gain the confidence of the majority and to lead them back to a place of genuine American values."

Mac was now completely speechless. As a tremendous flash of lightning was quickly followed by a deafening thunderclap, Danie suggested pausing for a while and just sitting together. Mac agreed, and they sat without speaking again until the first rays of dawn began to break through the dissipating overcast, welcoming a calmer, more gentle day.

# CHAPTER 7
## DAY 1

The morning was a spectacular demonstration of nature's order and beauty. The storm had ceased a couple of hours ago and the heavy wind and rain bowed to clearing skies and a gentle breeze. Mating loons cried their eerie song, and everything seemed at peace in the world except for Mac's poor mind, which was still in a mix of disbelief and awe. He tossed another log onto the campfire and prepared a fresh cup of coffee for himself and his new acquaintance. Danie broke their silence and said, "That was quite a storm."

"That was quite a story," Mac replied.

Her beautiful blue eyes were gentle but sincere as she continued, "Mac, I know that what I told you last night was tough to hear and tougher to believe." She lifted her coffee and sipped from the tin cup. "Wow, that's great coffee," she offered. "Can I continue, or do you have questions that need to be asked first?" Mac smiled and gestured for her to proceed. "Let's begin by considering a few things. Let's just assume that I'm telling you the absolute truth, and let's assume that my motives are good and geared to protecting a wonderful way of life. In the very near future America is going to devolve into something that is unimaginable by people of your time. You've watched the degradation of morality, integrity, and family values but you always believed that things would self-correct. They always do, right? Well, that's wrong! There exists, at this time, a very powerful and evil people who have been planning the alteration of the United States and the entire world into a world reliant on and controlled by them. The fact is that the more government controls the media, makes the general population dependent on it, degrades morality, specifically the basic family nucleus, and incites disharmony, the greater its power becomes. This group is a global enterprise whose sole interest is their own wealth and power. I know that you are acutely aware that these things are true and that it's the exact reason that you've returned to this place of order and serenity. You're searching for an answer, and you've returned to a place where life exists as it was meant to." Her monologue was interrupted by the piercing scream of an eagle not more than 100 yards from them.

"If you're telling me the truth, then why are you telling me?" Mac quipped. "I'm nobody and you seem to need a leader, a politician, someone smart enough to set things straight again."

"The answer to that question, Mac, is the very fact that you're here looking for answers that can't be found in the confusion of daily life outside the wilderness. The eagle that we're watching will dive on and kill a fish for nourishment. It doesn't kill for power or revenge; it simply kills and eats for survival. There is no animosity and no judgment. It's pure and simple. Conversely, the wilderness creatures have no empathy for other creatures, and that, my friend, is the basic difference between animals and humans. Humans have the capacity to care and feel for fellow humans. Our intellect gives us the capacity to act in the better interest of others, but this inborn morality is being destroyed by a constant barrage of disinformation from the media. Do you think that a group of people raised without outside influence would bear any prejudice based on skin color or any other physical or emotional differences? No, they wouldn't because there would be no basis for prejudice to exist. From the beginning of time, of course, there has always been social influence. Prehistoric tribes had leaders; eventually, more structured governmental entities continued to understand that control of the populus was to their benefit. So, man, right from the beginning, has subjected himself to the power of influence. That being said, the very basic morality inherent in everyone has been a force for good and the opponent of oppressors. It's been kind of a balance between good and evil if you will. Today, the balance is favoring evil, and we have decided that despite the risks, we would at least make an effort to reset the balance. When I say we, I mean a small number of people who have survived the oppression of evil that exists nearly everywhere in my time and have developed the means of trying to help, have elected to send a messenger back to possibly make a positive difference."

"This is more than I can digest all at once," Mac said, almost unemotionally. "Let's tap the brakes and hit the lake to catch some breakfast. Let's just be two people on a beautiful lake for just a little while... okay?" Danie smiled that breathtaking smile and agreed.

They paddled out to the mouth of the inlet, where the stream flowed into the lake over a shallow sandbar. The water was only about four feet deep, and in the morning and evening, the brookies, which are much better eating than the lake trout, rose to snatch emerging flies and other tidbits carried by the stream. Mac saw a nice rise and artistically dropped a muddler minnow (small deer hair floating fly) directly over it. No sooner had the fly touched the surface than a nice brookie gulped it down. As he played the hard-fighting trout, his mind wandered.

*What if she's telling the truth*, he thought. He couldn't help agreeing with the insane direction the country was taking. The president had lost any confidence of the general populace, except for the minority who, for some mad reason, refused to acknowledge his lies and apparent corruption. For more than half a century, Joe Biden had proven to be an arrogant, untruthful, and corrupt man. He was on the wrong side of every major decision with which he was involved. His family had profited unfathomably by selling political influence on bad foreign actors, yet the media had always seemed to support and cover for him and his family. *Why*, Mac wondered. He was corrupt, and like his former White House partner, Barack Obama, he appeared determined to fundamentally change the fabric of America. Why would a group of powerful people want to change the formula that was the cornerstone of the greatest country in the world? Mac figured that it made no sense except that the often talked about 'Deep State' (According to an American political conspiracy theory, the deep state is a clandestine network of members of the federal government (especially within the FBI and CIA), working in conjunction with high level financial and industrial entities and leaders to exercise power alongside or within the elected United States government.

The term 'Deep State' originated in the 1990s as a reference to an alleged longtime deep state in Turkey but began to be used to refer to the American government as well, including during the Obama administration. However, the theory reached mainstream recognition under the presidency of Donald Trump, who referenced an alleged 'Deep State' working against him and his administration's agenda. The use of Trump's Twitter account, combined with other elements of right-wing populist movements during his presidency, gave birth to numerous conspiracy theory groups, such as QAnon.

The term has precedents since at least the 1950s, including the concept of the military-industrial complex, which possesses a collection of generals and defense contractors who enrich themselves through pushing the country into endless wars, which is not restricted to the U.S. but was, in fact, striving for a central world power that could exert devastating control over the general populus and provide wealth and power to the few. He considered that such a concept was biblical in scope. The Bible predicts that toward the end days, there will emerge a global leader who all will follow but who is, actually, the antichrist. The thought of that beginning to happen in current times horrified Mac. The nice two-pound brookie was now close enough to net and put on ice, and Mac snapped back to the moment.

Danie had been quiet while he fought the breakfast fish, but she said, "Things are so beautiful here. We just can't let all this go without a fight, Mac."

They were returning to the campsite, and he replied, "What do you mean?"

"I can't reveal much about what we saw transpire because it's too dangerous for you to know the specifics of your future. I know that my just being here poses a huge threat to the space-time continuum, but we assessed that a nudge in the right direction is worth the risk. It sounds crazy, I know, but it's the truth." As the canoe met the shoreline, Mac wondered if his thoughts about world dominance and its relationship to biblical predictions were more factual than he wanted to believe.

The two made their way to the fire and Mac prepared the fish with some bacon and home fries for breakfast. Complemented by a welcome hot coffee, it made for a pleasant time. While they ate, Danie continued, "In my time, this kind of place no longer exists. The only knowledge of such complete peace and safety is what is learned from old reports, books, and, more recently, our ability to view the past through time manipulation."

"You mean that in such a short time, we've done that much damage?" Mac uttered in a clearly shaken voice.

"Yes," she replied.

"So. Assuming that you're for real, what do you figure to do to correct our course and why, again, are you here with me?" Mac queried.

"We can't, actually, do anything. All we can do is give you a nudge in the right direction. Do you remember what you said at your golf clubhouse last fall about politics and the existing border and gang issues?"

"No, what do you think I said?' Mac returned.

"Remember that I told you that we can now view past events in time? We observed you purporting this: 'The open borders, and I was an immigration officer, can't be allowed to pour millions of undocumented and unvetted illegal immigrants into the country. Not only is it in violation of our existing laws, but it's dangerous. There are cells established right here in our country and we have no means, under current administrative policies, to do anything about it. If I were president, I'd declare gangs and drug dealers domestic terrorists. Think about it, they're killing huge numbers of people, enslaving hundreds of thousands more in human trafficking enterprises, and prohibiting good people from enjoying the right to freedom and safety that the Constitution says we all have the right to enjoy. Once these groups are designated domestic terrorists, I'd use the might of our military to surgically strike the cartels right in their home bases. Most people have no concept of the sophistication and might of our military resources. I'd hit them hard, and, yes, there would be collateral damages, but that would be on them. It's time we protected our own. Then there are the gangs that steal from, hurt, and generally terrify everyday people. These gangs think that they're badass and pretty much untouchable. Well, they haven't seen what a Joint Special Operations (JSOC) (The Joint Special

Operations Command (JSOC) is a joint component command of the United States Special Operations Command (USSOCOM) and is charged with studying special operations requirements and techniques to ensure interoperability and equipment standardization, to plan and conduct special operations exercises and training, to develop joint special operations tactics, and to execute special operations missions worldwide. It was established in 1980 on the recommendation of Colonel Charlie Beckwith in the aftermath of the failure of Operation Eagle Claw. It is headquartered at Pope Field in Fort Liberty, North Carolina. For example, if you pick any city and any powerful gang, we tell them they have one day to stand down and disband, and if they refuse, and they will, we deploy a team with all the cyber, air, and land support at our disposal. It would be over in the blink of an eye. Once that group was totally decimated, we went live and warned all gangs and cartel operations inside the country that they also had twenty-four hours to pack up and leave or face the same retaliation. After a few strikes, they will cease and desist. They're evil but not stupid. Next would be the Islamic terrorist cells, who, unlike the cartels, are waging a religious war and are not afraid to be killed. These are tougher enemies, and the only answer is to give them exactly what they preach—death. Let the people of the country watch all that and then lead them in restoring dignity and integrity to our branches of government through the correct process of electing men and women who actually serve in the best interest of their constituents and to support and defend our Constitution. Finally, the decisive influence of the media. Once the people, all the people, realize how corrupt things have become and how quickly some of them are corrected, good old capitalism will do the rest. The media will quickly lose viewers, and since money drives that industry, they'll be brought into line quite quickly. The whole racism thing that's been fueled by the will of the few will settle down. Nobody, not black or white or any other ethnicity, wants to live in a world full of hatred and fear. We're all people, and we all want, basically, the same things. Respect, safety, prosperity, and a peaceful existence. It's not a difficult concept to grasp, and it would come around in no time.'"

"Do you remember the reaction of every single man and woman present? They exploded in support and said that they'd elect you tomorrow. You're a man with enough history and common sense as well as academic accomplishments to be the leader that is needed to correct the ship, Mac." Her voice ended in a very humble tone.

He remembered the talk and began to believe that she was being honest because how else could she have known such specific details about an unremarkable day a year ago. "That's pretty scary stuff, Danie," Mac said. He was becoming drawn to this girl because of the situation but also because of her beauty and character. She seemed to be a perfect complement to him, and she had a gently but fiery sparkle in her eyes and her smile.

The morning was moving along at warp speed. It was coming at noon, and it seemed like the entire night and morning were just a blur. The day had warmed, and the sun was hot on the calm, pristine water. The shore of the northern campsite was a shallow sand bar that extended out into about five feet of water before dropping off to deeper water.

"What do you think?" Mac asked. "Wanna take a swim and relax a little?"

Her more serious expression melted away into a girlish smile. "Sure, but I don't have any swimwear. There's no outdoor swimming where I'm from," she spoke in a teasing manner.

Mac visibly blushed and he was uncertain what to say. "We're here to save the world, and we're both adults, so what the hell, let's go for a swim the way we were created." She chuckled. Now, Mac was completely taken aback, but he figured that considering the storm of crazy things that were happening, why not. "Okay," he said, and they both began to undress together. She appeared to be completely comfortable, but poor Mac was as nervous as a cat on a hot tin roof. Danie was magnificent: her body was slim and toned, and her skin was almost olive and breathtaking. She had beautiful, smallish breasts crowned by gorgeous, well-defined nipples that made Mac begin to show signs of physical arousal. Maybe the cool water will slow things down, he thought.

She took his hand in his, and they waded into the clear, cool water. Mac was in a state of confusion, arousal, and worry all at the same time. He had never experienced anything like this in his nearly seventy years on earth. Danie appeared to be in her early fifties, but it was very difficult to be certain. They waded out to about five feet of water and then just folded into each other's arms. The morning was like something described by a poet. Words just couldn't do it justice. "Do you think you'll help me, Mac?" Danie said, moving her face closer to his.

"I'm sure willing to give it a try," he answered, and then she leaned in, and when their eyes were only inches apart, he kissed her gently at first, but when she responded, it became a deep and passionate thing. "I'm sorry," he said.

She gently touched his lips with her fingers and said, "I'm not. I've never experienced anything like this in my life. I'm not sure what's right or wrong, but this feels completely right to me." They continued to explore each other's cool, wet bodies while occasionally having to remember to actually breathe. In about twenty minutes, the quite cool water forced the two to return to shore. They both wanted the physical intimacy to continue, but Mac suggested tapping the brakes (he couldn't believe he said it) and getting dressed. She agreed, and once they were dressed, Danie said, "I think that we should share this campsite, Mac. We have a lot to discuss, and there isn't any sense in sleeping a quarter of a mile apart, is there?" Mac agreed, and the rest of the day was spent breaking her campsite down and moving it to his. During the move they didn't delve very deeply into her mission, and they simply enjoyed the picture-perfect day and each other.

As evening approached, they found themselves cuddled by the fire, watching, and listening to nature morph from day to night. They heard the last splash of a few trout feasting on evening flies, the eerie cry of a loon settling in for the night, the howls and screams pack of close-by coyotes embarking on their night hunting, and watched the moon rise, providing a surreal glow to the night sky that ushered in the completion of nature's transition. "It's more beautiful than I could have ever imagined," she said in a tender tone as she held Mac's hand and snuggled in a way that was completely foreign but as natural as breathing for her.

"Yep, it's pretty special," he answered. They remained by the fire for a long time before retiring to Mac's tent where they crawled into the two down sleeping bags that they had zipped together to make one suitable for a newfound couple.

# CHAPTER 8
## DAY 2

As the morning began to break, Mac, after very little sleep for the second consecutive night, crawled out of the bag and, after relieving himself, began to get a fire started so he could start brewing some morning coffee. It was another great dawn, and although physically tired, his mind was on fire. *Who is this mysterious woman and what, in the name of all that's holy, is happening and what's going to happen*, he wondered. He couldn't help reviewing the speech that Danie had quoted from the clubhouse over a year ago. He was speaking from the heart, but there was bourbon reducing his inhibitions and fueling his desire to just get it off his chest with the company of friends. Still, what he said had been genuinely how he felt. Obviously, the actions that he purported would have been the result of deep study and analysis. These actions just spoke to the defining dysfunction and disorder that the country was experiencing. The Biden administration had been preaching unity and order, but the fact was that it actively and deliberately promoted division and disorder. The administration courted the general, liberal media and blatantly encouraged support for racist and amoral concepts. People were being identified by race, creed, and color rather than being identified by character, integrity, and accomplishments.

As the fire began to crackle, Mac was reminded of a mission in 2017. Mac had volunteered to assist FEMA along with nearly twenty thousand other federal employees. Most of the season's damage was due to hurricanes Harvey, Irma, and Maria. Another notable hurricane, Nate, was the worst natural disaster in Costa Rican history. These four storm names were retired following the season due to the number of deaths and amount of damage they caused. Collectively, the tropical cyclones were responsible for at least 3,364 deaths. The season also had the highest accumulated cyclone energy (ACE) since 2005 with an approximate index of 224 units, with a record three hurricanes each generating an ACE of over 40.

Mac was deployed to Georgia for initial training and then traveled to Puerto Rico, followed by a boat ride to St. Croix and then on to St. Thomas to engage in the very first assistance and recovery efforts by FEMA. He was housed on a cruise ship contracted by the United States and roomed with a guy I'll call Pie Pan (a term used by Texas law enforcement officers to describe their distinctively large badges). Pie Pan was a big black guy whose real federal job was in information technology. He stood well over six feet, and Mac and Pie Pan looked like Bud Fisher's iconic Mutt and Jeff comic characters, except that Mac was white and Pie Pan was black. The berth they shared was very small, and it would take a couple of understanding guys to live together in such close quarters. The ship was fully staffed, and the facilities were open and offered to FEMA volunteers at half cost, so Mac and Pie Pan took advantage of the top deck bar to get acquainted. On the first evening, the two guys began what would become a lifelong friendship. In many ways, they couldn't have been more different. Mac was a Republican, and Pie Pan was a Democrat, for starters. They were of different ethnicities, and they were raised in completely different parts of the country. Donald Trump was the incumbent president, and the race for the 2020 White House was on, with Joe Biden being the favored Democrat. Pie Pan expressed a strong dislike for Trump, and Mac was equally opposed to a potential Biden presidency. It was a recipe for a strained relationship at best, but that wasn't how things shook out in the long run.

Over the months spent together in sweltering temperatures, working mostly outdoors for twelve hours a day, and sharing quarters that would test the patience of even best friends, the guys grew to respect and understand each other. Conversations were frank and open, personal feelings were shared (not jammed down each other's throats), and tolerance grew into understanding and acceptance of opposing ideas. Acceptance that everyone is entitled to an opinion and respect developed because both guys were able to argue their position in a nonhostile manner. Obviously, politics was often discussed, and Mac's position was that, although Trump was admittedly a loud narcissist, the collateral influence of his administration favored the best interests of our country. Pie Pan, on the other hand, favored a future Biden administration and was adamant that Biden would unite the country and promote the strength and morality of the United States on a global scale.

By the end of the deployment, the two new friends had learned a lot from each other, and above all, they parted as friends who agreed that people need to actually listen to and consider opposing positions rather than argue blindly in support of their existing positions. Thinking back, Mac chuckled because, not long after Biden took office, Pie Pan texted him that he was wrong about Biden and the incumbent Democratic party. He also referred to one particular incident from the deployment that both guys laughed about to the current day: Mac and Pie Pan, after long days of working, often partook on the reduced-price bar on the top deck of the ship. A fellow volunteer who stayed in a berth not far from them and who served on the same team was a hideously unattractive lesbian with a mouth more foul than any sailor, who Mac called Nooo. Nooo was a hard worker and got along great with the team, but she had absolutely no filter with respect to the words that came out of her mouth. One evening, Mac and Pie Pan were drinking heavily, and the rum and coke were having quite an effect on Mac and the rest of the gang. Mac, who never danced, was out on the floor shaking it up in style. He apparently had lost all his usual inhibitions, and everyone was blowing off steam in a big way. After his stint on the dance floor, Mac returned to the bar where Pie Pan was also taking a break. Out of nowhere, Nooo walked up to Mac and said, "I'm gonna make you my bitch, dance with me, too." Mac, as drunk as he was, stopped dead in his tracks and just uttered, "Nooooooo."

Well, Pie Pan just about busted a gut laughing, and then Nooo, in a much more passive voice, said, "Why, I have feelings too, ya know." Pie Pan ran interference and got his buddy back to their berth without incident.

Back in the room, Pie Pan said, "That was the funniest fucking thing I've ever seen. I never would have believed that you could be made speechless, but Nooo did it for sure." The men spent a long time laughing and just started saying "Nooooo" as a trigger to gut laughs. The expression has continued to provide laughter to the current day.

The thing to be taken from the entire deployment, Mac thought, was that people from any background can and should take the time to listen to one another and be willing to accept that their preciously held opinions might just be wrong. At the very least, they should understand that varying positions are, generally, based on life experiences and deserve to be considered. The current Biden administration was pushing for the exact opposite. They appeared to promote gender and race identity rather than evaluation based on a person's accomplishments and personality, and they seem to be encouraging disharmony and intolerance. *It's just wrong,* Mac thought as he snapped back to the fire and Danie.

Danie emerged from the tent, and the morning sun illuminated her beautiful smile. Even in jeans and a flannel shirt and with no makeup, she was, without question, the most beautiful woman Mac had ever laid eyes on. "Mornin,'" she said as Mac offered her a steaming hot coffee. "God, this place is more beautiful than anyone could ever describe. In my time, this beauty is gone forever, and it's probably the greatest cost of man's mistakes that will ever happen." Although Mac found it nearly impossible to comprehend, he nodded in agreement.

A pair of otters were splashing around just offshore, and what looked like play was simply these two creatures fetching breakfast from the lake, just like Mac and Danie. The two looked into each other's eyes for a long time before Mac broke the silence by saying, "Now what?"

Danie said, "I guess the ice is broken, so now it's up to you to decide whether or not you'll accept the challenge and allow me to guide you toward protecting everything that you hold valuable."

Still completely unsure, Mac said, "I don't think that I have a choice. Tell me, is what happened last night just part of your plan?"

"No," she replied in an almost shy tone. "It wasn't even considered. For me, this is all new ground. Not just the travel to another time but meeting you. I'm having feelings that I've never experienced, and it's all making me understand how desperately important my mission is. What is happening between us is new and exciting for me and I hope that you feel the same."

"Same here," Mac responded. "So, now what?" he asked. Danie told Mac they needed to get back to the real world sooner rather than later and get to work on establishing Mac as a nationally recognized figure. One who would offer the people of the United States a chance to usher in a new and powerful force for correction. Again, Mac was dumbfounded.

The day was warming up and the air was clean and provided a wonderfully soothing effect. Danie sat quietly, allowing Mac to process her message. "Okay, you're the one with the plan. How do you see this playing out?" Mac was deadly serious, and all his senses seemed to be on fire. It was something like being in a firefight: terrified but fully focused on the mission and the events unfolding at warp speed. In a fight, the noise is deafening \but here on the lake, it was the quiet and peace that was imposing. Mac knew that it was time for action, but despite his wide-ranging experience he was completely unsure of exactly what the next step should be. This was completely new territory for the old soldier, and it made him very uneasy.

"Here in this idyllic place, it seems that we have all the time in the world," Danie put forth, "but the reality is that the next election is only a little more than a year away, and we have a lot to accomplish in that space of time. I think that we should pack up and head back to civilization without much delay. I'll continue to fill you in as we travel."

Mac's mixed emotions were fogging his ability to focus. He was falling for this strange, beautiful woman in a way he had never experienced but at the same time, he was mesmerized and terrified at the same time by the message she brought. He walked over to his pack and fetched a bottle of Four Roses bourbon. He returned to his chair and poured a cup for Danie and one for him. "I think I need to regroup, Danie. Let's have a snap and do some mission planning." Going off halfcocked is a recipe for disaster, he thought, so stepping back, assessing the situation, exploring options, and deciding on a course of action seemed to make sense to him. Granted, the best plans are not developed while drinking, but shit, this whole deal was completely off the books anyway, he figured.

"Deal," she said and accepted the drink. One drink led to many more, and as the two basked in the warm sun and gentle breeze, they continued to talk. Danie expounded a little about what prompted her mission. Apparently, from her time perspective, it was clear that evil forces had been deliberately undermining the moral correctness inherent in most people. Granted, there had always been extreme cases of immorality and bizarre actions but those had always been very few, while the vast majority of people were generally guided by a more noble standard, a sense of right and wrong. Although people vary significantly in their ideology and purpose, they value kindness, integrity, and family as imperative cornerstones of their specific societies. Certainly, there had always been harshness and evil, but like in nature, it all seemed to find a reasonable level in the end. In more recent history, especially in the United States, people were being deliberately divided through messages delivered through the media and taught in our educational system. It was to the point that children in elementary school were being forced to address their sexuality and ethnic origins, which were becoming the basis of personal evaluation rather than the nature of an individual.

Previously, this would have been deemed child abuse and simply not tolerated, but morality was becoming blurred at an almost irreversible rate. The very heart of our system of government and justice is being increasingly weaponized to promote the purposes of the few and to punish and silence anyone who dares to voice an opposing position. In Columbia, Missouri, on October 30, 2008, on the cusp of his historic presidential election, Obama stated, "We are five days away from fundamentally transforming the United States of America." Those words were then and still now frightening. The fact that he planned to transform our country begs the question: transform it into what?

He succeeded magnificently. He weaponized the Department of Justice and used it as his personal tool to squash any opposition. He used the Internal Revenue Service's power and scope to hunt down and punish anyone who voiced an opposing position, and he used the Federal Bureau of Investigation to further spread disinformation while again punishing any and all significant dissidents, especially Donald Trump, who won the election in 2016. Trump suffered brutal attacks from every branch of government and especially from the government-controlled liberal media that pressed a constant barrage of blatantly false information as well as disinformation designed to keep the general populous in check. Trump narrowly defeated the liberal champ, Hillary Clinton, and on his first day in office, he began to dismantle Obama's chaos and reestablish the American system that the people had elected him to protect.

With no prior government or military experience, Donald J. Trump stunned the world and critics when he defeated former U.S. Secretary of State Hillary Clinton in the 2016 U.S. presidential election.

In the four years he stayed in power, the Trump administration typically pursued trade protectionism, a plethora of deregulation exercises, and individual and corporate tax reforms. These policies, in so many ways, caused the federal budget deficit to balloon. For those on the left and critics of the president, Trump's political and economic initiatives (i.e., America First) were too anti-global in nature. However, the upside of those policies (conservative legislation and ideals) resulted in remarkable economic growth and close to full employment in the U.S. Trump irritated many people with his name-calling and constant tweets, but the net effect was positive, and the country was slowly returning to its former self.

From day one when Joe Biden was elected in 2020, he compiled a list of monumentally disastrous moves, including, first, of course, the withdrawal from Afghanistan. Biden pulled out our troops before getting out our civilians, green card holders, and allies, then had to send troops back in to help them get out. Yet even then, Biden failed to get everyone out despite promising to do so. In addition to stranded people, the evacuation left billions of dollars' worth of arms, vehicles, and equipment in the hands of the Taliban, abandoned a strategic base in the fight against terrorism, and allowed the release of imprisoned hard-core terrorists.

Another Biden disaster happened at the southern border. The number of illegal immigrants that streamed into the country this year, all because of Biden's refusal to enforce our immigration laws, is stunning. That number includes thousands of so-called amnesty seekers, who are generally released into the country with an order that they show up for a hearing in the distant future—an order that often goes ignored. It also includes people who are unvaccinated or infected with COVID-19, as well as gang members, drug traffickers, sex traffickers, and even individuals on terrorism watchlists. The president's primary duty was to "take care that the laws be faithfully executed." Biden has willfully failed to do so. That is an impeachable offense.

Right up with these two disasters is that of inflation. Prices are rising steeply, with no end in sight. On top of what already amounts to a cruel tax on the poor and those on fixed incomes, Biden wants to spend trillions more, which will just make inflation even worse. Moreover, the economy is suffering from massive supply chain bottlenecks, with ships waiting weeks to get into ports and a shortage of workers and truck drivers to deal with them once they get in.

A principal cause of the current inflation is high energy prices—the product of Biden's energy policies. Upon assuming office, Biden immediately canceled the Keystone XL pipeline, which would have employed some 11,000 people. The oil that would have come through the pipeline will still come in, though by costlier and more polluting means (trucks and rail). At the same time, Biden gave his approval for the Nord Stream pipeline from Russia to Germany. At the same time, he was restricting domestic oil and gas production, leading to higher gas and heating prices; Biden called on OPEC and Russia to supply more oil and gas in order to reduce those prices.

Biden has fully embraced identity politics in the federal bureaucracy. Many of his appointees have been selected based on their race, sex, LGBT status, and so on, and not because they were the most qualified persons available. Biden has also reinstated critical race theory training for federal employees. His administration thus reinforces rather than rebuts the poisonous lies now spread throughout our educational system and in the body politic.

Another Biden failure has been his mishandling of the COVID-19 pandemic. Biden inherited the enormous benefit of coronavirus vaccines produced by the Trump administration's Operation Warp Speed. His response to the COVID pandemic thereafter has been characterized by frequent policy reversals. The most recent of which is the unconstitutional ordering of vaccine mandates—a move that, previously, the president said he would never make. As a result, the country is faced with the resignation and firing of police officers, firefighters, health care workers, and armed forces personnel. Even worse is that, despite the availability of vaccines, more people have died of COVID-19 during Biden's presidency than during Trump's.

Biden has thoroughly politicized the enforcement of federal law. His Justice Department fails to treat equal offenders equally. It meted out harsh punishments and lengthy pre-trial detentions to those who, on January 6, broke into the Capitol, few of whom engaged in any violence or destruction of property. They were, at most, guilty of trespassing and obstructing a governmental proceeding, offenses which have been frequently committed by left-wing groups (recall, for example, the Kavanaugh hearings). Contrast the treatment of the January 6 defendants with, for example, the DOJ's treatment of Antifa and BLM rioters who tried to burn down a federal courthouse in Portland, a much more serious federal crime. And now the DOJ has turned its attention to parents complaining about schools' racializing and sexualizing their children.

The military has been similarly politicized under the Biden administration. Its function is to be a lethal threat to foreign adversaries, not a political partisan or a social experiment in woke ideas. But the generals and admirals in charge know that the Biden administration is in thrall to identity politics; so, to further their careers, they bring woke concepts into the military at the expense of its basic function. And with respect to that basic function, Biden—while backing major spending increases in many domestic programs—has left the military with a reduced budget, in terms of purchasing power. At the same time, our adversaries are rattling their sabers.

Finally, it is worth commenting on Biden's character. Biden is prone not just to embellishing the truth but to outright lying. His campaign lied about his son Hunter's laptop—saying that well-substantiated reports of its contents were Russian disinformation. He lied about Hunter's business dealings, including possible influence peddling, with the Chinese. He lied about what Donald Trump said regarding the Charlottesville protests. He lied about Kyle Rittenhouse, claiming the teenager was a white supremacist before his trial even began. Throughout his political career, he has plagiarized and told whoppers about things he was supposed to have done (but didn't do).

Mac's head was swimming and not from the copious amount of bourbon the two shared during Danie's monologue but because everything she addressed resonated deeply with the old soldier. They lapsed into silence and sat listening to the peaceful lapping of the gentle waves on the sandy beach and bathed in the pure serenity that was Allagash Lake. Finally, they moved from the fire to the tent and drifted off into a deep, peaceful sleep in each other's arms. Mac's uncertainty was washed away, and a new and firm resolve to do his damnedest to help his new friend accomplish her mission. The last thing he remembered was Danie's warm body next to his and a sense of purpose that was unlike anything he ever experienced.

# CHAPTER 9
## LEAVING THE LAKE

Although Mac usually woke up before dawn, when he first opened his eyes, it was already a bright new day. He threw on some clothes and ventured out of the tent to deposit his morning flow. It was cooler with a light southwest breeze, which suited the northeast trip up the stream to his truck. After getting a fire started and putting on the coffee, he sat and watched the lake. He couldn't help but wonder how man had made such a mess out of something so magnificent. In the wild, it just felt right, whereas back in civilization, life had become complicated and often dangerous. He considered that despite the problems in society most people still retained a sense of morality and family values. They were basically good people, but they were being inundated by subliminal messaging as well as overt messages designed to alter their basic good nature. Something had to be done, he thought, and maybe, just maybe, Danie was the answer.

He called Danie, who was still sleeping, and told her that the coffee was ready. In short order, she emerged from the tent and, like Mac, headed to the bushes to relieve herself. When she returned to the fire, she gratefully accepted the coffee and said, "How are you feeling today?"

Mac was more deliberate this morning and answered, "I think that we should pack up and head out today. If everything that you've said is true, then we have a very tight window of opportunity. It's already June, and the election is a year from this November and as elections go, that's very tight, especially for an unknown candidate. I think that we should only take what we can safely carry in one canoe and stow the rest with a note containing my contact information and that an emergency forced us to leave in a hurry." Mac hated to ever leave anything behind in the wilderness, but he knew that the warden service would pack the gear out and he'd be slapped with a significant fine, but all things considered, that was an acceptable scenario. They ate a small breakfast and packed everything they weren't taking out in a tight bundle covered with Mac's tarp. They broke down Danie's camp in a similar fashion, and by noon, they started the four-hour trip upstream to Mac's truck.

The current wasn't very strong, and most of the trip could be paddled, but there would be a few shallow spots where Mac would have to get out and drag the canoe and others where the current was stronger, and the elevation dropped more sharply where he would have to pole the canoe. Poling was a method of moving your canoe upstream in fast water by standing and using a cut pole to push the canoe along. It's a skill mastered by the early loggers in the North Maine Woods but only practiced these days by a few. Having two paddles did make the effort less arduous, though.

As they approached the first beaver dam along the route, Mac motioned to Danie to be quiet. He heard some splashing up ahead and didn't want to make the turn and come face to face with a cow moose with a calf or two. Most of the year moose and bears were no concern in the wilderness as they wanted no part of humans and usually vanished into the bush long before you got close enough to see them. But, in the spring, they often had young with them, and that changed the dynamics significantly. A cow moose was probably the most dangerous animal in Maine when defending her young. Beaver dams were ingenious creations that backed up sufficient water to provide a deep enough pond for the beaver to build a house accessible from underwater but allowed them to emerge inside. The dam allowed sufficient water to flow through so the stream or brook's flow wasn't significantly disturbed. Just downstream of the dam the water was, generally, a bit more shallow than the overall brook depth.

As they turned the bend, Mac realized that the splashing wasn't the moose he anticipated but, rather, a sow black bear with two cubs. They were about 100 feet from the bears when they rounded the turn in the brook, and the water was only a foot and a half. Mac stopped the canoe and told Danie to be still and quiet. The big sow came up on her two hind feet as the cubs played in the water like kids do. The sow's eyes were fixed on Mac, and her nose was on high power. A black bear's sense of smell was the best in the animal kingdom. In fact, they could pick smells up to a mile away. She was in protection mode and God help anything that threatened her cubs. The rule of thumb regarding black bear encounters was to give the animal space and make a lot of noise, so it realized it was unwelcome. This bear was defending cubs, so the game was very different. Mac had decades of experience in the Maine wilderness, and he had a special connection with animals. He wasn't afraid, and the bear was acutely aware of that. He wasn't aggressive and that also was imparted to the huge bruin. He spoke to her softly as she slapped the water and snapped her teeth in defiance. Then she bawled at the cubs, never taking her eyes off Mac, and, like kids, they ignored her. Suddenly, she slapped one of the cubs and sent it rolling in the water. At the same time, she barked loudly at them. Well, that worked because both cubs bolted out of the water and up a nearby fir tree. Once they were safely up the tree, she dropped down and followed them. Mac and Danie sat quietly until he saw the trio move off into the forest like a silent shadow.

Finally, after about a forty-five-minute delay, they got out and dragged the canoe up over the dam and continued upstream. Danie told Mac she was terrified the whole time and that all of her training for the trip had never prepared her for something like what they just experienced. Mac chuckled and explained that it was no big deal and that it was a perfect example of how things worked in the wilderness. "There is a balance that is always maintained unless it's interfered with by humans. I'm not saying that things always turn out nicely in the wilderness. There are fires, there are daily encounters that become savage and deadly, and there are always horrific results from extreme weather, etc., but in the wild, these anomalies are smoothed over time, and the balance of order returns every time. With people, things don't follow any sense of normality. People affect incidents based on emotion or greed or even because they have been programmed to act a certain way, often without even realizing it. Emotion and greed have always been part of the human psyche, but deliberate behavior modification is very new in the scope of human history. It's motivated by the very few by the old desire for power and wealth, and it's become systemic in most cultures, but in America, it's at a boiling point. For generations, we have been programmed to embrace ideologies that contradict our natural instincts. The core family values are being destroyed. Accountability for our actions is disappearing, and we're being turned against each other based on race, religion, and political views. Sure, people have always been more comfortable with others who look and act the same but the reaction to differences is becoming extreme and encouraged. People always warred with other tribes or cultures, and this is the result of basic human desire for power and wealth but in olden times, the norm was that people didn't kill or maim without perceived gain. I guess this is still true because even the apparent wanton crimes committed by gang members are committed because the individuals believe there is a benefit to their actions. Maybe it's acceptance by their gang or some monetary benefit, but only insane people commit acts with absolutely no sense of an apparent good resulting from the act. The problem today is that we're being conditioned to accept a narrative that is designed by a few very evil characters as opposed to the inherent, albeit flawed, nature of our species. I'm sorry, I shouldn't rant like that," Mac said. Danie just nodded, and they continued upstream.

The remainder of the trip was peaceful and calm. Late in the afternoon, they arrived at the landing where Mac's truck was parked. It had been a rugged trip as far as physical exertion was concerned, and after stowing the gear, they set up the tent, gathered some firewood, and then made their way down to the stream to clean up. It was a very warm evening, and they undressed and waded into the four-foot-deep water. The bottom was mostly sandy, and the cool water felt wonderful on their bodies. Every time Mac saw Danie's naked body, it took his breath away. She was the most beautiful woman he'd ever seen, and her smile was intoxicating. He came close to her, cupped her face with his hands, and stared deeply into her eyes. Her smile morphed into something more sensual, and it stirred Mac emotionally and physically. They kissed slowly and for a long time, and his clear physical arousal was evident. She softly said, "Let's head up to the tent." That's exactly what the two did and for more than an hour, they became all consumed with each other. It was something that transcended anything Mac had ever experienced.

As evening slowly transitioned into nighttime, Mac kindled the fire, and the two sat and listened to nature, making her magnificent swap from day to night. They were sitting, just holding each other, and not even speaking when the relative silence of the night was pierced by the distinctive "hoo hoo hoo hoo hoo hoooo ah!" of a barred owl. Mac said, "Watch this." With a chuckle, he responded to the owl with a very similar call. Almost immediately came a response, but from a different direction. Then, the night was broken by the calls of several more owls. "This is gonna be crazy," Mac whispered. Suddenly, the night erupted into what sounded like a tribe of monkeys screaming at each other (a distinctive interaction by these silent nighttime creatures). It went on for twenty minutes, then as suddenly as it began, it stopped.

"That was crazy," Danie said.

"Yep, one of my favorite wilderness experiences," Mac replied. Shortly after, they turned in for the night, and they both drifted off into a remarkably peaceful sleep.

Dani's eyes cracked open, and she sat straight up in the sleeping bag, startled by a very loud hammering sound just outside the tent! Mac had already gotten up and was somewhere outside. She called to him, saying, "What's that noise?"

Mac laughed and said, "That's just a pileated woodpecker." The pileated woodpecker was one of the biggest, most striking forest birds on the continent. It was nearly the size of a crow, black with bold white stripes down the neck and a flaming-red crest. "He's right out here, come on out and have a look." She threw on her clothes (less shoes and socks) and popped out of the tent. Mac pointed to a big dead tree right on the side of the stream.

She was, once again, awestruck by the sight of this magnificent creature. "It's beautiful," she muttered, and, in a moment, it was gone.

"I wish that everything in the world was as perfect as it is out here," Mac mused. Having said that, Mac considered the volume of mystical and inspiring places he'd been, and he continued, "I'd love to show you many more places and things, kid. We could spend a lifetime just wandering and exploring."

"That would be magical, and as much as I'd love to ignore my mission and just escape with you, we have a job to do, and if your kids and their kids are ever going to have a chance to be free, happy, and able to experience these things we must get to it!"

"Yep, I reckon you're right again. Hey, breakfast is ready," Mac said as he offered her a hot cup of coffee. She accepted the steaming cup and sat by the fire to have breakfast that consisted of eggs, bacon, and biscuits made from scratch back at the lakeside camp. Everything tasted, smelled, and felt better here, she thought. It was a cooler morning, but the sun was bright, and the gentle breeze carried the wonderful smells of the spring woods.

After eating, they cleaned up the gear, packed everything into his truck, and headed west back to what some referred to as the real world, which, oddly, was the exact opposite of how Mac viewed things. Danie had never ridden in a pickup truck on dirt roads and, like everything she was experiencing, it was a new adventure. Heading east toward Ashland, Maine, they were looking at a five-hour trip. The sun was directly in their faces, and Mac offered his new friend a pair of sunglasses. He chuckled because even these old, beat-up glasses looked magnificent on her. They rode with the windows down and continued to discuss the mission. About an hour into the trip, she noticed a large dark animal several hundred yards ahead. As they closed the distance, she realized that it was two animals, not one. "This is gonna be good," Mac said softly. When they closed to about one hundred yards, it became clear it was a pair of new moose calves. Suddenly, from the right side of the dirt road, a huge cow exploded out of the thick cover! She landed on the gravel, her ears pinned back and her hair standing straight up on her neck. Although most of the time, a cow moose appeared docile and avoided any contact with humans, when she was protecting her calves, she was one of the most aggressive and dangerous animals in North America. Today, however, the kids bolted across the road and disappeared in the heavy forest and once she was comfortable, they were safe, she followed. Standing nearly seven feet at the shoulder, she presented another breathtaking scene for Mac's new friend. "Does it ever stop being so exciting?" she asked, and he just smiled and continued driving.

They arrived at the Ashland checkpoint (gateway to the North Maine Woods) around 6:30 p.m. and decided to continue some thirty more miles into Presque Isle to get cleaned up and enjoy a sit-down meal. They settled into one of the few hotels in Presque Isle and after showering, they put on their cleanest clothes that still smelled like campfire smoke and headed to a local restaurant for a couple of drinks and a meal.

"It's so very different from where I'm from," Danie mentioned. "Things seem so relaxed and peaceful that it's hard to understand the turmoil that we know exists in your time," Mac explained that Presque Isle was a very small city and, although on the surface it appeared nice, over the past twenty years, things had changed dramatically. For example, when he moved here in 1971 no one locked their homes or vehicles. Often men would leave their trucks running during very cold weather while having breakfast in a local eatery. Camps were never locked, and most had a note on the table stating that, in the event of an emergency, anyone was welcome to use the place and asked to treat it as if it were their own, and that was exactly the way it would be done. Today, low employment and drug use have changed everything. Camps were often vandalized, and homes were broken into regularly. Petty crime was rampant, and drug running was common. Accountability for actions, especially among the young, was nearly nonexistent and discipline in the schools was so restricted that acting out and blatant disrespect for teachers was the rule rather than the exception. The older folks tried to hang on to their tried and tested way of life, but it was becoming a losing battle, and this was rural, small-town America. The larger cities were beginning to resemble war zones, with gangs battling each other openly and crime at unprecedented levels. Men, women, and children were being killed daily, and local governmental authorities were actively advancing policies that protected the criminals rather than the victims. Policies such as Critical Race Theory differed from academic understanding of critical race theory from representation in recent popular books and, especially, from its portrayal by critics often, though not exclusively, conservative Republicans. Critics charge that the theory led to negative dynamics, such as a focus on group identity over universal, shared traits, divided people into "oppressed" and "oppressor" groups and urged intolerance.

CRT was an example of a deliberate attempt to change the fundamental values that America was built on. It served the elite and powerful minority's desire to break down the existing society by infusing values that led to division and mistrust among the population. By creating dysfunction, lack of accountability, and dependence on governmental support, the will of the population became increasingly easier to mold.

Gender identity indoctrination was becoming an increasingly serious issue in elementary schools. There was a growing consensus among teachers that was driven by policies underwritten by the teachers' unions and other more nefarious entities that children as young as nine years old should be forced to consider gender identity and that their parents were not to be included in decisions made by the child at school.

Gender identity was once just a fringe concept of postmodern philosophy. Today, it is regularly causing real-world harm to children and teenagers (particularly girls) across the country in sports, schools, and even youth camps. The blatant promotion of transgenderism had infiltrated schools without parental consent and at the expense of academic learning. Gender identity school policies and practices were becoming widespread. Curricula, books, videos, and activities promoting the transgender ideology were used with students as young as age five. It was common, moreover, for these materials used with students to contain sexually explicit content. Parents were intentionally left in the dark by school personnel about the sexual content taught. Often, parents only found out about the inappropriate content from their children, who were confused and distressed about what they had been taught at school. This preoccupation with gender identity indoctrination was, moreover, at odds with the reality of biological sex and had several harmful long-term effects on children.

Gang activity in the United States was at epidemic levels. Some 33,000 violent street gangs, motorcycle gangs, and prison gangs are criminally active in the U.S. today. Many are sophisticated and well-organized; all use violence to control neighborhoods and boost their illegal money-making activities, which include robbery, drug and gun trafficking, prostitution and human trafficking, and fraud. Many gang members continue to commit crimes even after being sent to jail.

According to the United States Department of Justice, *"Gangs are associations of three or more individuals who adopt a group identity in order to create an atmosphere of fear or intimidation. Gangs are typically organized upon racial, ethnic, or political lines and employ common names, slogans, aliases, symbols, tattoos, styles of clothing, hairstyles, hand signs, or graffiti. The association's primary purpose is to engage in criminal activity and the use of violence or intimidation to further its criminal objectives and enhance or preserve the association's power, reputation, or economic resources. Gangs are also organized to provide common defense of their members and interests from rival criminal organizations or to exercise control over a particular location or region.*

*"Gangs develop and maintain perpetuating characteristics including manifestos, constitutions, and codes of conduct which provide an identifiable structure and rules for initiation and advancement within the association. Through their use of open intimidation and identifiable insignia, gangs may be distinguished from other organizational criminal groups such as La Cosa Nostra and transnational criminal*

*organizations who rely on secrecy and clandestine control of legitimate businesses and governments to advance their criminal aims.*

"*This study of gang members' criminal activity considers the general community impact, violent gang criminal activity, gang members returning from prison, gang migration and immigration, gangs in schools, and the economic impact of gangs. Since the impact of gangs is notably worse in the more densely populated areas (50,000 and over), this bulletin focuses on youth gang impacts in these areas. For these areas, the impact of youth gang activities encompasses the intimidation of other youth, adults, witnesses, and business owners. Once the large number of gang-related homicides in Chicago and Los Angeles are taken into account, just over one-fourth of all the homicides across the country are considered gang-related. Gang immigration may be a factor of greater importance than gang migration in the impact of outsiders on local gangs. Gangs in schools are likely underestimated. Generally, law enforcement agencies tend to under-report gang incidents, and their estimates of the number of gangs and gang members are likely to omit a substantial number of students. Gangs tend to influence youth to become career criminals whose lives involve multiple arrests, convictions, and periods of incarceration. A single adolescent criminal career of about ten years can cost taxpayers between $1.7 and $2.3 million. The Comprehensive Gang Prevention, Intervention, and Suppression Model (Spergel, 1995) is a flexible framework that guides communities in developing and implementing a continuum of programs and strategies for countering the adverse impact of youth gangs.*"

This cancer that is metastasizing in our country is, actually, domestic terrorism. According to Wikipedia: *"Under the 2001 USA Patriot Act, domestic terrorism is defined as "activities that (A) involve acts dangerous to human life that are a violation of the criminal laws of the U.S. or of any state; (B) appear to be intended (i) to intimidate or coerce a civilian population; (ii) to influence the policy of a government by intimidation or coercion; or (iii) to affect the conduct of a government by mass destruction, assassination, or kidnapping; and (C) occur primarily within the territorial jurisdiction of the U.S." This definition is made for the purposes of authorizing law enforcement investigations. While international terrorism ("acts of terrorism transcending national boundaries") is a defined crime in federal law, no federal criminal offense exists which is referred to as "domestic terrorism." Acts of domestic terrorism are federally charged under specific laws, such as killing federal agents or "attempting to use explosives to destroy a building in interstate commerce." Some state and local governments in the United States do have domestic crimes called "terrorism," [8] including the District of Columbia."*

Also, the critical open border policy of the Biden Administration has become a matter of national security. According to the Heritage Foundation, "Two of Joe Biden's immigration policy reversals have even created national security risks. His decision to lessen the protection of our southern border has allowed a massive influx of illegal aliens, drug dealers, human traffickers, and, quite possibly, terrorists. And by abandoning Trump's merit-based immigration reform initiative, Biden has hobbled the U.S. in its technology race with China—something that carries undesirable economic and military consequences."

An open border is a serious national security risk.

Open borders, where illegal aliens can cross with relative impunity, invite criminal activity. The flood of illegal border crossings since Biden has taken office is unprecedented. According to U.S. Customs and Border Patrol, monthly arrests at the border now number in the hundreds of thousands, a thirty-year high. Criminals are among those caught at the border and then released. Many other criminals evade law enforcement at the border and enter the interior as well.

The Biden administration has adopted dramatically restrictive policies for law enforcement agencies whose mission is to remove these criminal and illegal aliens. Officers have been instructed to essentially turn a blind eye to many people who have no right to be in the country, including those who have been ordered removed by a judge. In May, deportations dropped to the lowest level on record.

The illegal population in the U.S. could expand by millions in Biden's first year in the Oval Office—the direct result of Biden's unfortunate policies. The administration has already encountered over 1.7 million at the border, a figure that does not include those who just slipped in unnoticed.

Weak border security and nonexistent interior enforcement, combined with promises of legislative or "de facto" amnesty, create powerful incentives for aliens to flock to the border and attempt to enter illegally. They feel they have a good chance to enter, remain and work in the U.S. without fear of expulsion, and also hold out hope for American citizenship.

The security consequences of porous borders and a broken and unforced immigration system are manifold. The impact on transnational crime is the most obvious. Illegal aliens are victims of a myriad of crimes, from rape and robbery to human trafficking.

Further risks come from the control of the cross-border activity by cartels. According to research by the Department of Homeland Security, about fifty percent of border crossers in the 1970s used the service of smugglers. Today, that number is over ninety-five percent. Human smugglers charge thousands to tens of thousands of dollars per person to make their trek across the border. Under Biden, the cartels have made unprecedented profits.

The cartels then use these profits to finance other illegal activities. For example, the cartels are responsible for smuggling most of the fentanyl entering the U.S. This fueled the opioid addiction and drug overdose epidemic in this country.

The terrorist threat is even more serious. Groups like ISIS and al Qaeda remain our enemies, and U.S. defense and intelligence officials have warned of a resurgent transnational terrorist threat after Biden's chaotic and calamitous withdrawal from Afghanistan.

Terrorists could dispatch a team to the U.S. to stage an attack on the scale of 9/11. Today, the best way to infiltrate a team into the U.S.

would be by crossing the porous southern border, hiding among the vast numbers of people crossing our border illegally."

Mac realized he had been talking for a long time and apologized for his rant. Danie simply smiled in agreement, and they finished their meal without delving deeper into political or social issues.

Back in the room, they settled in and continued the discussion about what needed to be considered moving forward. Danie was enjoying a glass of Chardonnay, and Mac sipped his Four Roses bourbon (neat with an ice cube). Clearly, time was a critical factor. It was late June, and if the plan was to have any chance, Mac needed to get on the presidential ballot by late summer. Getting on the ballot is no small task! The paperwork alone is monumental, and the requirements are daunting. Money is another critical consideration. Being a completely unknown candidate would require an extensive and well-prepared introduction via social media, television, radio, and face-to-face appearances.

Provided the financial obstruction was taken care of (which Danie seemed certain about), they would have to assemble a team of experts as advisors, and it had to happen sooner rather than later. They would need a campaign manager who understood the unique nature of this effort, one or two military experts (probably from Joint Special Forces Command (JSOC) and another from executive military operations like the joint chiefs), a representative from the intelligence community such as senior executive from the CIA, a domestic law enforcement professional such as a senior FBI agent, a constitutional expert, an accounting and legal team, an information technology (IT) wizard who was an expert with social media and website development, and, yes, a political expert who understands the intricacies of the political world (legitimate and nefarious). No worries ... LOL

It was approaching midnight, and the couple decided to call it a night, so they climbed into bed, and their attention turned to each other and more immediate physical and emotional satisfaction. It seemed like they were becoming more like a unit than two separate entities, and that was a wonderful experience.

# CHAPTER 10
## BACK TO NEBRASKA

The trip from Presque Isle to Lincoln, Nebraska, is about 1,800 miles, and they planned to make one overnight stop in Indiana. The conversation on day one centered around the requirements to enter a presidential election and a first draft of how to accomplish getting on the ballot. Mac was no expert in the process and Danie was reluctant to take the driver's seat for reasons she chose to keep to herself.

Mac proposed that the first issue would be financing and offered that he had absolutely no idea where to begin securing financing. Danie suggested they put the financing matter on hold until they were back in Nebraska but didn't offer any reason why or suggest whether she had ideas or knowledge that might be helpful.

Mac indicated if they assume that financing will be obtained, he figured that the assembly of a team would be the next logical step. He proposed that the first team member must be someone with knowledge of political processes, and he had a friend who might either fill the role or suggest someone who could.

For political matters, Mr. Jim Burbank (Jake). Jake was an unimpressive figure of a man. He stood five foot nine inches, was balding, and carried about thirty extra pounds. Just your average guy except for his eyes. His powder blue eyes were piercing. They weren't the beautiful Paul Newman blue eyes. Rather, they were almost startling with an effect that made you feel like he was peering directly into your soul. It was a somewhat unsettling effect despite his amicable personality. He was one of those people who was easy to like, and he had a sense of humor that was contagious.

Mac met Jake while posted in St. Thomas, U.S. Virgin Islands, in 2017. Jim was the assistant director of operation for St. Thomas during the deployment, and because Mac was an expert in writing macro-enabled spreadsheets with embedded interactive reports, he spent many hours working with the director and Jim, streamlining their reporting efforts. Mac and Jim became good buddies over a couple of months they served together with FEMA. The two had remained in regular contact ever since. Jim holds a Harvard Master of Business Administration (MBA) degree and, among his other work accomplishments, served with the United States State Department Diplomatic Affairs Division in an executive capacity. Most recently, he worked as a senior campaign team member for the last Republican president.

For a consultant regarding military matters, Mac suggested Colonel Mark Evans (call sign Osprey). Mark is a West Point graduate and a graduate of the United States War College. After graduating from Ranger School, he was accepted and completed The United States Army Special Forces (SF), colloquially known as the Green Berets, due to their distinctive service headgear, which is a special operations force of the United States Army.

The Green Berets are geared toward nine doctrinal missions: unconventional warfare, foreign internal defense, direct action, counterterrorism, counterinsurgency, special reconnaissance, information operations, counterproliferation of weapons of mass destruction, and security force assistance. They're capable of hostage rescue and combat search and rescue if needed. The unit emphasizes language, cultural, and training skills in working with foreign troops; recruits are required to learn a foreign language as part of their training and must maintain knowledge of the political, economic, and cultural complexities of the regions in which they are deployed.

Mark joined JSOC Joint Special Operations (JSOC) in 1985 and served as a Commanders of Combatant Commands until his retirement in 1998. The Command (JSOC Joint Special Operations) is a sub-unified command of the United States Special Operations Command (USSOCOM). It is responsible for studying special operations requirements and techniques, ensuring interoperability and equipment standardization, planning, and conducting special operations exercises and training, developing joint special operations tactics, and executing special operations missions worldwide. The chain of command for military operations goes from the president to the secretary of defense to commanders of Combatant Commands. The chairman of the Joint Chiefs of Staff as an intermediary, transmitting orders between the secretary of defense and the commanders of Combatant Commands.

Mark and Mac met in North Africa while serving together during Operation Eagle Claw. They became close friends and have remained so.

In the matter of Information Technology (IT), including social media applications development and use, Mac thought Pete Farnsworth would be an excellent choice. Pete was an unusually tall man with a slight frame. Standing six-foot-six inches, he weighed only two hundred pounds. He wore glasses and had a pale complexion despite living right on the Atlantic Ocean. Mac met Pete in 1998 while attending a conference in Boston, Massachusetts, where developers were discussing possible programmatic problems that could occur as the new millennium began in 2000. During the three days of intense, high-level discussions, Mac and Pete formed a bond and kept in touch ever since.

Pete holds a Master of Media Arts and Science degree from the Massachusetts Institute of Technology (MIT). He spent many years as a senior consultant to Google, specializing in new media platform development and management. An expert in accounting and finance would be a critical team member, and Mac figured that Dr. Mason DeWitt might be the ideal candidate. Mason earned a PhD in Accounting degree from Stanford University and passed his Certified Public Accounting (CPA) exam. The two met through Jim Burbank in 2002 and worked together on several of Mac's business development programs, including a revolutionary five-year, interactive program that produced detailed pro forma financial statements for customers seeking financial aid for their projects. Mason served as the Finance Director on the campaign team for a former democratic president.

Finally, Mac needed someone to advise on international affairs and Dr. Michelle Jolicoeur was his clear choice. Michelle holds a PhD in International Economics from Cambridge University in the United Kingdom. She was a senior consultant to the Vice President of Budget Performance Review and Strategic Planning at the World Bank for many years. Now retired but still conducting selective consulting activity, she met Mac in 1979 through Scottish in-laws and has remained a trusted source of advice over the years.

Back-and-forth discussions about the proposed team members and the advantages they all offered continued for the remainder of the trip home. Mac and Danie arrived in Lincoln in the late afternoon of the second day of travel, and after unloading his jeep, they drifted into more personal discussions over some Château Montelena Napa Valley Chardonnay until the physical exhaustion caught up with them, and they elected to hit the hay for a well-deserved night's sleep.

# CHAPTER 11
## FINANCING SOLVED

Mac, as usual, was up, showered and making the morning coffee around sunrise. Danie was still enjoying a great night's sleep. While pouring through the pile of mail on his desk, he was stunned by a letter from McInnes Cooper of Moncton, New Brunswick, a law firm specializing in international estate matters.

The letter was a request for Mac to travel to Moncton, New Brunswick, to address the matter of a deceased client from the United Arab Emirates. The letter suggested that the client has bequeathed a significant fortune to Mac upon verification of his identity and acceptance of several terms outlined in the estate. No mention was made of the specific description of the wealth or the terms. Mac immediately responded to the phone number included in the notification, and the company confirmed the authenticity of the notice and requested that Mac set a date for his appearance. First-class travel arrangements would be included for Mac and any associate(s) he deemed necessary. He told the firm representative that he needed to consult with his significant other and that he would call back later in the afternoon.

Danie was slightly taken aback by Mac's demeanor when he woke her. He was visibly shaken and excited. Over coffee, he presented the letter, which she read carefully. "This has nothing to do with my mission, at least not anything that I'm aware of," she said. Max explained that he had no idea who this deceased client was or how he was involved.

Time was critical to their mission, but they both agreed that pursuing this notification might be advantageous, and they decided to accept the invitation and travel to New Brunswick as soon as possible. Mac called the law firm back and arranged to travel to Moncton in three days.

They departed Omaha, Nebraska, that Thursday and arrived in Moncton in the early afternoon. They were met at the airport by a representative of the form and were driven to the offices in downtown Moncton. At the offices, Mac and Danie we treated like royalty, which neither could understand. They were ushered to a conference room and provided refreshments. The room was staffed by several well-dressed men and women, typical for Canadian business professionals, who came to the point without delay.

During a deployment in North Africa, Mac had taken action that saved the life of a young man who as it turns out, was the son of the firm's client. Mac recalled the incident, which at the time didn't register as anything out of the ordinary. It happened during a covert reconnaissance mission in Tongo, Niger. Mac was embedded with a few other air traffic controllers to provide assessment and establish extraction logistics for the team. In military tactics, extraction (also exfiltration or exfil) is the process of removing personnel when it is considered imperative that they be immediately relocated out of a hostile environment and taken to an area either occupied or controlled by friendly personnel. In this case, the team established a primitive runway that would accommodate the team and the cargo they were protecting. During the operation, they were attacked by hostile forces, and a fierce firefight ensued. During the fight, a young Arab man who was operating as part of the team was shot and would have been killed if Mac hadn't risked his own life by emerging from cover and dragging the soldier to safety. Mac sustained a hit in the side during the effort, but the bullet passed clean through without damaging any vital organs. The operation was completed; all team members and cargo were extracted, and Mac was flown to Germany for medical treatment and debriefing before returning to his home base in England. He never gave much thought to the young, wounded soldier.

That young man was the son of one of the wealthiest UAE men of the time. He had been providing assistance for the United States Delta team as an embedded expert. The client used his influence to discover the identity of the soldier who saved his son's life, and this gift was his way of expressing his gratitude.

The attorneys further explained that the terms of the transaction were that the identity of the benefactor, as well as the details of the action in Africa, must remain secret, and a document to that effect must be effected. After agreeing to the terms Mac was told that the amount of the gift was one billion U.S. dollars. Mac almost fell out of his chair. That amounted to more than six hundred million dollars after taxes and other miscellaneous expenses. Mac and Danie completed all required actions and instructed the firm they would be in touch with information about their United States law firm and banking details shortly.

They departed New Brunswick the following day and returned to Nebraska. When Mac and Danie got back to Mac's place, it felt like the world was spinning out of control. They rested for a day and the following morning, they decided to begin executing the mission, but first Mac needed to engage a top-notch law firm and enlist the services of a CPA company as well. After several days of research that included many conversations with friends and colleagues, Mac settled on a Portland, Maine law firm that was recommended by one of Mac's old friends who served as a secretary of defense under a past Republican president. The attorney assigned to Mac suggested a top-six accounting firm to handle the specifics of money management.

Mac instructed his attorney to contact the Canadian lawyers to accommodate the deposit of the recent gift into a fund established by his new accounting company. Nearly six hundred million dollars would be available to Mac in no more than a week.

Having these details completed, Mac felt that the mind-bending surprises were over, at least for a while, and he breathed easier. The relief, however, was short-lived. At breakfast, Danie handed Mac a power ball ticket she purchased while they were traveling from the lake back to Nebraska. Mac said, "Thanks," but paid little attention, considering the ridiculous odds of ever winning these things. He considered lottery tickets 'The State's Tax on Stupidity' and always felt it was an abuse of the people who bought them the most frequently but could ill afford them.

"Just for chuckles. Check them numbers... okay?" Danie asked. Mac smiled and obliged his new best friend.

When Mac looked at the winning numbers for that draw his heart felt like it stopped beating, then jumped into hyper-gear.

He stared at the numbers on his computer and back at the ticket several times before he said, "Holy shit... is this for real?" The ticket matched all the online numbers, including the multiplier. Danie was smiling like a Cheshire cat, and Mac somehow knew she was more than casually aware of the outcome. "Did you have anything to do with this and the gift from the UAE?" he asked.

"My team, in my time, was aware that we would need financing to proceed with the mission, so I was given numbers we knew were winners. I have no knowledge about the UAE gift. That must have been solely the result of your actions in Africa."

Mac's mind was swirling because the value of the winning lottery ticket was another nine hundred million dollars that would provide over four hundred million dollars after taxes and miscellaneous costs. They now had more than one billion dollars to use in their effort to accomplish the mission they had embarked on.

After verification of the winning number, Mac instructed his accountant to add the new cash to his existing portfolio with the exception that one hundred million dollars was to be placed into a trust for his five children and another six million to be issued to each child and his ex-wife in equal amounts immediately.

Mac and Danie had been working without much rest since they decided to leave the lake and undertake the mission. They had established a list of potential team members, resolved the financial requirements, and secured legal and accounting professionals. They decided the next step would be contacting and securing members of the team who would then become invaluable sources of guidance and support. First, though, the two decided that a week to unwind was a great idea so they planned a working vacation to Thailand. Mac always loved Thailand with its beautiful coastal bungalows in the south and, his favorite, visits to the magnificent northern mountains with their ancient temples and cool azure waterfalls hidden deep in the forest and away from the general tourists. He knew the right people to contact, and the trip was booked.

In the meantime, Mac reached out to his old friend Jim Burbank, who was living on Cape Cod, Massachusetts, and enjoying his retirement. After explaining what had transpired and the current mission to get on the 2024 ballot as an independent, Mac asked Jim if he'd be willing to run the campaign. Poor Jim's head was swirling like a leaf in a Texas windstorm, and rightfully so. Jim had complete confidence in Mac, but this news was tough to swallow. He told Mac he had to take some time to digest everything, and Mac suggested he run out to the Cape to sit down and talk about it, and Jim agreed.

Immediately after confirmation that the money from the UAE benefactor was available, Mac bought a Cessna Citation X jet and hired a citation pilot named Stan, who Mac knew well and trained with years ago. The Citation is a corporate jet that seats up to twelve passengers and cruises at over 500 nautical miles per hour (KTS) with a range of more than three thousand miles. He selected it because it's an extremely stable aircraft and he had done some training in one. The decision to buy versus leasing or flying commercially was made because Mac knew that travel would be frequent and spontaneous during the campaign.

Mac called Stan and instructed him to have the jet ready for a flight from Lincoln to Hyannis in the morning. Stan, now on salary and staying in a local hotel, agreed.

# CHAPTER 12
## OFF TO THE CAPE

The next morning Mac and Danie flew to Hyannis and were met at the airport by Jim. Jake, as Mac called him, drove them to his home in Chatham. Jake had a beautiful beachfront home that overlooked Ryder's Cove, where Mac often put out during his time commercial fishing with his old friend Paul back in 2005. Jake was married, and his kids were all up and out, enjoying successful careers of their own. Jake's wife, Katie, a lovely auburn-haired lady with piercing green eyes, brought drinks out to the deck, and they all sat to discuss the mission. Mac went through everything that had happened so far with Danie filling in about the bizarre nature of her presence and mission. After a few hours of catching up and pouring over the plan, Jake, with Katie's blessing, accepted the offer to Mac and Danie's relief.

The group enjoyed a wonderful evening meal that Katie whipped up and continued talking while the sun set over the relatively calm ocean. The view and the warm salt air breeze were another new sensation to Danie's senses. They all called it a night around 2200, and all had a tough time getting to sleep despite the calming sound of the surf and the successful outcome of the meeting.

In the morning, Mac and Jake were the first to rise, and over coffee on the deck, they continued the planning. Jake offered that time was critical to comply with all the registration requirements. For independent candidates who meet the age and residency requirements, the next step in the ballot access process typically involves collecting a certain number of signatures from registered voters in the state or county you hope to serve. Independent and third-party presidential hopefuls must petition each state to be included on the national ballot.

Jake asked how Mac intended to introduce himself to the country considering that he was a complete unknown. Mac suggested that he contact Pete Farnsworth, who was also retired and living in Rockland, Maine, which was only a few hours' drive or a fifteen-minute flight away. Jake agreed, and Mac called his old friend immediately. Fortunately, Pete answered the call, and Mac asked if he and Jake could run up to discuss a time-sensitive and critically important project. Pete said he was busy for the next three days but happily agreed to meet the next day. Mac told Stan to have the jet ready in the morning of the third day for a flight to Augusta, Maine, for four passengers (pax).

Over breakfast, the group decided to relax and have some fun for a couple of days. Jake had a beautiful Bertram 50S fishing boat, and they decided to spend a couple of days on the water. Mac suggested they ask Paul to captain the boat so they could relax and continue discussing the plan. Jake knew Paul and agreed immediately.

Mac called his old buddy, who was more like a brother, to ask if he'd be willing to drive the boat for them. Paul and Mac grew up together in a small Massachusetts town. They lived less than a half mile from each other and spent a good part of their youth fishing and hunting together. Paul spent a year in Vietnam in 1968 where he served as a machine gunner. He carried the venerable M-60, a belt-fed machine gun, and earned two purple hearts for injuries sustained in battle and both bronze and silver stars with valor for heroism under fire.

After the war, Paul and Mac married sisters, so they always called themselves brothers-in-law. Paul was divorced early in his marriage and moved to Cape Cod, where he pursued his dream of fishing for a living. It was a rough road at first. He slept on the deck of his small center console boat when he couldn't afford to rent a dry place to live. During that time, Paul became an expert saltwater fisherman and captain. He landed more than twenty giant bluefin tuna alone with some exceeding one thousand pounds. These fish are powerful beasts and can swim nearly fifty miles per hour. Paul used to say that hooking one was like tying into a Volkswagen with fins. A fight would often last more than four hours, and only the most determined and physically powerful men could handle the battle successfully. Paul was a magnificent specimen of a man. He stood six-foot-three inches with broad shoulders and a narrow waist. He was an athlete par excellence from the time he was a young boy.

Mac and Paul enjoyed many hunting trips together, and one always came up as stories were told over drinks. It was the early seventies, and Mac was stationed in Northern Maine as an air traffic controller. He was recently divorced from his first wife. At the time, Mac was a young airman who was carrying sixteen hours per semester and maintaining a 4.0 grade point average while working full-time as a controller, which was no small task on its own. The couple had two children, and his young wife became dissatisfied with Mac's attention to school and work, which left her with no social life. Mac was working to earn his bachelor's degree and obtain a commission with the goal of becoming an Air Force pilot. The marriage failed in 1976, and Mac never finished or earned his commission. It was a bad time in his life, to be certain.

Paul drove up with another mutual buddy to cheer up his lifelong pal and have a hunt. It was early November, and deer season was just beginning. The weather had been quite warm, with no snow yet for tracking. Mac brought the guys to one of his favorite spots, a ridge that looked down on the Aroostook River, where a densely covered flat piece lay between the river and the ridge. Mac put Paul and Danny on runs down in the flat, and he settled three-quarters of the way up the 1,500-foot ridge. Mac parked himself on the side of a power line that ran from the top of the ridge all the way to the flat. It was a mix of soft and hardwoods and a great place to catch a deer crossing from the cover on one side to the deep woods on the other. It was a warm morning and Mac got nestled in just before daylight. He sat quietly for about an hour and a half, just enjoying the magical smells and sounds of the world transitioning from night to dawn.

He almost nodded off because he was enjoying the peace and not tremendously worked up about shooting a deer that morning. His peace was shattered by a man calling to him from just below his perch. "You gonna' shoot that bear?" the man shouted as he pointed up the hill behind Mac. The guy was dressed in buckskins, more like the attire of a hunter from the seventeen hundreds. At the same moment Mac heard something running down the hill behind him. He swung around to see a huge black bear barreling down the power line straight at him. He only had time to shoot from the hip, and as the Winchester 30-30 cracked, the bruin let out a roar and plowed right through Mac driving him ass end over the tea kettle to the ground. It all happened in a flash, and as Mac sprung back to his feet, he looked for the odd man who had called to him. There was no one there so Mac eased down to the exact spot where the guy was standing. It was a muddy spot where a rivulet of water surfaced from beneath the ridge. Mac was already an excellent tracker, but he could see no evidence of a man having stood there. No tracks in the muddy ground, no snapped twigs or flattened grass... nothing! He was shaken and confused. It just didn't make any sense.

Paul and Danny had no luck that morning, although Paul jumped a monarch buck in the thickest cedar swamp imaginable but never got to let a round fly from his Ruger .44 caliber carbine. When the three met up down in the flats, Paul announced that he thought he heard a shot and some kind of roar from up where he figured Mac was sitting. Mac explained the incident to Danny's amusement, but Paul knew his buddy and was as astonished as Mac was. The story became a must-tell on many different occasions.

Paul agreed to skipper the trip, and they arranged to meet at 0300. the following day at Ryder's Cove where Jake's boat was tied up.

It was a great morning, still dark but warm and calm with forecast seas to be southwest at five knots—perfect fishing weather. The five loaded their day gear onto the Bertram, which was fully fueled and ready to go. They eased out of the slip around 0400 and moved slowly out of the harbor toward the open ocean. Paul decided he'd take the new cut—a break in the sand bars that blocked direct access to open water because it was almost high tide—and the boat would negotiate the shortcut without the danger of running up on a sandbar just slightly submerged. Jake said that he would never try that on his own, but both men had complete confidence in Paul's nautical expertise.

They made it through the cut, and as they exited the rough waves that were always present between the cut and open water, they opened up, steering southeast to the commercial lanes about forty miles offshore to hunt for bluefin tuna. As they opened up, the sun appeared as a red ball that appeared to magically rise out of the ocean. The warm salt breeze and the magnificent view took Danie's breath away. She wondered how people could risk losing such beautiful and emotional experiences by succumbing to a deliberate and methodical plan to corrupt the very fabric of the country.

Cruising at a comfortable twenty knots, the ride to the planned fishing spot would take about two hours. Katie went below deck and whipped up a great breakfast for all. Paul just took a breakfast sandwich and a coffee at the wheel. After breakfast, Jake and Mac joined Paul in the wheelhouse (the area where the boat was operated from) and filled

Paul in on the recent events and the plan they were developing. Paul's head was swimming, which seemed to be the normal effect of the story.

An hour and a half out, Paul spotted a large flock of birds circling and diving off the bow. He suggested they make a run over to them to see if there were any mammals (whales or dolphins) feeding. Mammals were a good indicator that the bluefins were close by. All agreed, and they steamed closer to the birds. Paul didn't see any blows (water being blown out of a whale's head when it surfaces), but his ridiculously keen eye picked up something else. He shouted, "Get the girls and come see this." Everyone but Paul assembled on the stern (back) of the boat that was open for fishing. Paul slowed and inched forward, where the group saw a pod of orca (killer whales) in an unusual configuration.

They were moving in sort of an oval shape with cows and calves inside and a perimeter of what Paul said were males protecting the pod. Suddenly, a great white fin broke the water as he headed directly toward the pod, looking for a calf to snag. The boat was only about a hundred yards, and Paul said, "This is gonna' be great!" Danie was absolutely mesmerized as she had only seen videos of these magnificent creatures. Now, maybe fifty yards from the action, the shark slowly submerged. He was preparing to dive and come up from below. No sooner had his fin disappeared than the water exploded as a huge bull orca breached (came out of the water) with the two-ton fish in his jaws. The orca nearly cut the shark in two, and when the two crashed back into the water, there was nothing, but a red stain left to see on the surface. Danie was visibly shaking but before she could compose herself, the unexpected happened again. No more than twenty feet off the starboard (right) side of the boat, the huge male surfaced. He lay motionless and stared directly into Danie's eyes. The intelligence was as clear as the morning sky, and she felt as if he were assessing her. Apparently satisfied that the boat was no threat to his family he simply faded down into the sea and was gone.

"Ya don't see that every day!" Paul shouted. The stunned crew continued to the numbers (Global Position Satellite (GPS)) that Paul had set into the navigation system.

When they arrived at the numbers, Paul began to set up the outriggers. Outriggers are devices attached to a fishing boat's sides and extend beyond the hull. They are typically made from metal or plastic and feature a series of long poles that are adjustable to different lengths. The purpose is to provide stability for the fishing boat and a platform from which to fish. By extending beyond the hull, they help to prevent the fishing boat from tipping over in rough waters. In addition, outriggers provide a place to attach fishing lines, making it easier to cast out into the water. As a result, they are an essential piece of equipment for any fisherman.

He set the riggers and attached his hand-made squid rigs, which are a series of rubber lures that imitate squid in a diamond shape with only the trailing squid bearing a hook. Paul let out a port (left side), starboard (right side), and another directly behind the boat at about five to seven knots. He was seeing whales blowing and breeching, which was a good sign, but even better, he was seeing tuna directly below the boat at about fifty feet on the fish finder.

Everything since Mac met Danie had been unimaginable, and this fishing trip was certainly going to be no exception. Often, guys drag rigs for hours or even days before they get a strike, but not today. Not more than twenty minutes after the rigs were deployed, a giant (generally tuna over seven feet and more than six hundred pounds are considered giants) exploded out of the water directly behind the venter rig, and the sound as it crashed down on the trailing hook was like a plane crashing into the ocean. Paul called for Mac to take the wheel, and he sprinted to haul in the starboard rig while Jake muscled in the port. Mac had dropped the boat into neutral, and the reel was screaming as the thousand-pound monster made his initial run. Paul and Jake moved to the stern and Jake strapped into the fighting chair. The battle was on. Paul returned to the helm (steering the boat), and Mac moved to the stern to help Jake and call out instructions to his old buddy.

After the initial run, tuna are unpredictable, and keeping the line tight by controlling the direction and speed of the boat is critical. Jake had a steady fight for about thirty minutes, inching the line in by pulling on the line with a gloved hand and cranking the huge Penn reel with the other. It's a brutal workout, even for the most physically capable men. Suddenly, the tuna turned and headed for the boat, and the line went slack, so Mac shouted, "Running at us, full ahead." Paul responded, and in no time, Jake had a tight line again. The fish then made a run to the port, and Paul accommodated with expert maneuvering. Another long, slow fight finally exhausted Jake, and Mac took over. After two and a half hours of fighting the huge fish, Mac shouted, "Straight down...

harpoon time, Paul." Paul swapped the helm with Jake and scrambled down to the stern, where he prepared the harpoon.

A harpoon is a long spear-like projectile used in fishing to shoot, kill, and capture large fish or marine mammals such as bluefin tuna. It accomplishes its task by impaling the target animal and securing it with barb or toggling claws, allowing the fishermen or hunters to use an attached rope or chain to pull and retrieve the animal.

Mac fought the fish until it was only twenty feet straight down at which point Paul set himself ready to throw the harpoon. As soon as the tuna broke the surface, Paul launched the missile and struck the fish perfectly. Once the barb was firmly embedded into the tuna, Paul wrangled the attached line until the fish was losing some of its fights, at which time he handed off the line to Mac and prepared to tail wrap (getting a rope around the tail to finally subdue the fish) the monster.

Finally, the dead giant was hauled into the boat through a haul-in door (a small door on the back of the boat where large fish can be pulled in) and iced for market. This fish was around 900 pounds and would fetch a handsome price back at the fish market.

It was late afternoon when the group arrived back at Ryder's Cove, and by the time they secured the boat and gear, got the tuna to the fish market, and finally arrived at Jake's house, it was 2000. Paul had headed home, and the four were too exhausted to even consider going out to dinner, so they got cleaned up and enjoyed the sunset from Jake's deck over a light meal and drinks. The day had been nearly indescribable, and once again, Danie was amazed beyond words by the beauty and excitement she was being exposed to.

The following day was a kickback and relaxing time. The group discussed Mac and Danie's plan. Jake expounded, in some detail, that the process of getting Mac on the ballot was no small undertaking and that Mac would require a solid ground team as well as a powerful media presence.

He continued by explaining that even with sufficient financing, which Mac evidently possessed, the population had to be introduced to Mac, and he had to reach enough of them with a message that was stimulating enough to entice the voters to actively support him in a way that no other independent had ever successfully accomplished. No small effort, for sure.

Jake pointed out that, in his opinion, there were several specific issues that Mac must address with clear evidence of a plan to correct. According to Dr. Abraham Maslow, he explained, there is a basic hierarchy of human needs that drives all motivation except for abnormal psychotic considerations. He explained Dr. Maslow's theory to Mac and Danie in basic terms.

Maslow's hierarchy of needs, he said, is a motivational theory in psychology comprising a five-tier model of human needs, often depicted as hierarchical levels within a pyramid.

The five levels of the hierarchy are physiological, safety, love/belonging, esteem, and self-actualization.

Lower-level basic needs like food, water, and safety must be met first before higher needs can be fulfilled.

Few people are believed to reach the level of self-actualization, but we can all have moments of peak experiences.

The order of the levels is not completely fixed. For some, esteem outweighs love, while others may self-actualize despite poverty. Our behaviors are usually motivated by multiple needs simultaneously.

Applications include workplace motivation, education, counseling, and nursing.

Assuming that this theory is an accurate definition of what motivates people, it's fair to apply it to political motivation as well. People need to feel safe first and foremost. We are social creatures, and immediately after feeling secure, we need the emotional satisfaction of loving and being loved. Our self-esteem is tied directly with the first two and the entire hierarchy is a fluid concept that is driven by many factors. It's not like mathematics, where A plus B will always equal C.

Working on this premise, Jake proposed that several current situations directly affect the American population's perception of safety, security, and peace of mind. He continued by explaining that, despite the flood of intentionally designed media conditioning efforts, people have basic and unwavering needs that they don't even recognize consciously. This, he made clear, applies to all humans regardless of race, religion, or any other personal preferences.

How can people feel safe, he continued, when violent crime is unchecked? Even the fortunate few who live in reasonably calm rural areas are exposed, through television and social media, to the horrors of gang activity and organized violent looting. People are witness to millions of foreigners entering the country illegally, and they aren't foolish enough to accept that, at a minimum, a huge number of these foreigners are here for nefarious purposes. They watch daily reports of unwarranted attacks on innocent people, and they are made painfully aware of the inconceivable number of countrymen who succumb to drug overdoses daily. They feel the decay in the moral fabric of our nation at large that begins with the breakdown of the family unit. Despite being motivated to align themselves with a particular political party's rhetoric, they know, deep down in their hearts, that things just don't feel right.

Another situation, Jake proposed, that causes serious concern is global unrest. Folks are inundated with daily violence around the world. Despite the blame ascribed by the different political forces, the evidence is abundantly clear that the world is a powder keg, and the fuse is burning closer to the powder daily.

Added to all the aforementioned situations is the common person's sense of financial security. People are experiencing an almost unsustainable increase in the cost of providing food, shelter, and transportation. Again, the blame game is being delivered by the mainstream media, but regardless of the cause, the net effect is ever-present.

So, Jaked asked, how does an unknown candidate present himself to the American voter with a message that moves voters from their deepest motivational needs and makes them accept that he can and will enact the changes necessary to right the ship and begin to return the country to a place that satisfies peoples most sacred needs, needs that they do not consider consciously but needs that are ever present just the same? No small goal, to be sure!

# CHAPTER 13
## UP TO MAINE

The following morning the four new friends met Stan at the airport, and after a short, fifteen-minute flight, they arrived at the Rockland airport. Rockland is a small airport that lies just off the coast and has full Instrument Flight Rules (IFR) capability. This means that Stan can land Mac's jet in almost any weather conditions safely. Pete met the group at the airport, where Stan had arranged a Chevy Suburban for their use. They followed Pete to his oceanfront home which was only a twenty-minute drive. Pete lived alone, having lost his lovely wife to cancer several years ago. He had two boys who were grown and had families of their own who visited often and were his greatest source of happiness.

Pete's home is situated on five beautiful acres located on the northern edge of the town line. Like Jake's, his deck provides a spectacular view of the Atlantic and it rests some fifty feet above sea level. His property has three hundred yards of mostly rocky, rugged coastline. At the southern end of his property, however, he had a beautiful sandy beach that stretched about one hundred yards. The property sloped gently down to the beach, and he had installed wooden stairs to better accommodate the trail.

After introductions, the group moved to Pete's eastward, ocean-facing deck. He had mounted an old ship's wheel facing the sea, and Danie remarked that it seemed as if they were, actually, sailing a ship. Pete chuckled and told her that that was his intent when he had it installed. Pete and Jake had never met, but they quickly appeared to form a bond, likely due to their mutual love of the sea. Mac and Jake laid out the mission concept, how it came about, and some of the initial political hurdles that must be attended to in short order. The concept that Danie has arrived from a future time, of course, initially stymied Pete as it had everyone else on the deck. Maybe it was his confidence in Mac, or perhaps it had something to do with Danie's demeanor that evidenced her heartfelt devotion to her mission. Most likely, a little of each finally moved the big man toward acceptance of the tale. He was flabbergasted by Mac's sudden wealth. Another circumstance that would unsteady anyone.

Jack expounded on the specific capabilities that the new team considered Pete's area of expertise, should he decide to get on board. He explained that one of his most urgent objectives would be to acquire the required signatures in many states. He continued that since Mac was a completely unknown entity, they needed to introduce him in a new and powerful way to as much of the population as quickly as possible.

"Oh sure, no pressure. Just accept the whole mission from the future thing, conceive, create, and implement a brand-new method of introducing an unknown candidate, and accomplish all that in a completely unreasonable timeframe," Pete injected with a chuckle. He followed by pledging, without hesitation, that he was all in! He shared that he would need to recruit a few colleagues who each possessed specific unique skill sets in the IT field and were trusted friends. He concluded by suggesting that he would begin his assignment within the following few days, and Mac offered that no cost would be considered prohibitive, including the use of his jet or chartered aircraft to help Pete's team with logistics.

As the conversation continued over welcome cocktails, the mood turned festive, and Mac offered to prepare the evening meal. During their earlier fishing trip on Jake's boat, Mac and Paul detoured slightly on the way out and picked up a few nice striped bass (stripers). Striper is Mac's go-to seafood. They provide beautiful white flaky fillets that have a gently non-fishy meat. Mac also brought some oysters and scallops with him. Pete suggested that he call a friend at the local fish pier and have some fresh Maine lobsters delivered to complete the banquet ingredients. Amazingly, there were no arguments voiced.

Mac, who loved to cook, left the group, and headed for Pete's kitchen. Danie accompanied him. As they worked together preparing the feast, Danie confided to Mac that her confidence in the mission was growing by the day, and she explained that she had no idea that Mac had such talented and loyal friends. Mac told her that he assumed she had detailed information about everything, and she responded that her details about the past were not as clear or detailed as he imagined. For example, the winning lottery numbers were easily accessed, but individual relationships of non-public individuals were simply not available. Mas accepted her explanation and it added another level of understanding about the mission and his beautiful new companion.

Mac and Danie worked for a few hours in the kitchen, and it was a labor of great enjoyment for both. Finally, they announced that dinner was ready. Mac served lazy lobster (lobster chunks served in melted butter and seasoned with salt and pepper), lobster salad (appropriate for making lobster rolls), Oysters Rockefeller (raw oysters served on the half shell with a spicy cocktail sauce), bacon wrapped scallops, a vegetable medley, and the pièce de résistance, baked striper! It was truly a meal fit for kings. The new friends dined, continued to discuss the mission, and watched a magnificent sunset. Although the sunset in the west (behind them), the morph from day to night, as seen on the oceanfront deck, was almost a religious experience.

The gathering continued well into the evening and didn't conclude until after midnight when the two couples and Pete, on his own, retired to their bedrooms for a wonderful night's rest. The evening was cool with a slight breeze so Mac and Danie left the windows facing the ocean open, and the smell of the salt air and the gentle rumble of the surf was hypnotic.

With the exception of Mac, who was always an early riser, most of the group slept until nearly 1000. Pete was the next to rise and joined Mac out on the deck for coffee. Mac had already been down to the beach at sunrise and took a bracing swim in the cold Maine waters.

Mac and Pete were continuing their discussion about the mission when Danie appeared barefoot in jeans and a sweater. She took both men's breath away with her elegant and unpainted beauty, but her smile was her most intoxicating feature. Pete persisted in questioning his new friend about the mission and her knowledge of the future, especially matters of a technical nature. Danie understood his compulsion to gain insight, but she politely reiterated that according to rules designed to minimize her effect on the space-time continuum, they allowed for extremely limited discussion of such matters. Pete understood but couldn't hide his disappointment. Mac consoled his old buddy by reiterating that everyone involved so far had suffered similar frustration.

Finally, Jake and Katie emerged and joined the group. All agreed that yesterday, with its mission announcement, the introduction of new friends, and a meal for all times, would go down in the annals of their experiences as one of the most remarkable. Mac then suggested that with political and IT expertise established, his next contact should be his old JASOC buddy, Mark Evans. Mark was a bachelor who had retired from the military many years ago and now lived in Montana. He had a beautiful cabin situated in the Bob Marshall Wilderness (The Bob). The Bob is a vast stretch of land in western Montana that remains virtually roadless and with very few homes. Mark had secured an old ranger station in the more southern stretch of The Bob and converted it to a beautiful log home with million-dollar views. A veteran helicopter pilot, Jack kept his Robinson R66 helicopter hangered in a pole barn he built. The four-passenger chopper provided Mark a reasonable opportunity to travel down to Lincoln for supplies when required.

Lincoln was a VFR Airport that required a ceiling of 1,000 feet and visibility of three miles to land. This meant that trips to Lincoln had to be made in very good weather. If urgent travel was required Mark would fly to Helena airport that offered full instrument approaches. Mark enjoyed the beauty and solitude of the mountains and often shuttled a guest or two up to his place for visits.

All agreed, and Mac contacted Mark via email to arrange a meeting. Mark had Internet service through satellite service that was poor in bad weather but otherwise quite reliable. Later in the day, Mac announced he had heard back from Mark, who arranged to meet the whole team in Helena, where he would leave his bird and rent a larger helicopter to carry everyone to his mountain retreat.

# CHAPTER 14
## OUT TO MONTANA

The next morning the growing team met Stan at the airport and departed for Helena. Mac's jet was able to accommodate seven passengers in luxurious comfort, so the ride was very enjoyable. The jet touched down in Helena at 0230, and Mark was there to meet them. It was spring, and they had ample daylight on a bright, cloudless day, but Mark urged for a quick departure for the short flight to his place. All agreed, and they were off in less than an hour.

The flight to Mark's retreat was breathtaking. Mac was the only one of the group to have visited Mark's place and the rest were mesmerized by the vastness and beauty of the wilderness. They landed some fifty minutes after takeoff, and the old log cabin that most expected was, in fact, a sprawling two-story log home with horse stables to the east of the house. Mark always kept several quarter horses and a few mules. Inside they were stunned by the thirty-foot great room that was surrounded above by a railed second floor that overlooked the room. A stone fireplace extended the entire way to the ceiling, and it was adorned with luxurious leather furniture. Mark was an avid hunter, and the walls displayed several mounts, including a monarch bull elk, a few mule deer, and a full mount, standing grizzly bear. Mark had made very smart investments over his career, and they had rewarded him with a substantial retirement portfolio.

After introductions and the usual mind-numbing grapple with Danie's story, the growing team assembled on Mark's westward-facing deck. He selected the west-facing placement of the deck because he reveled in the stunning sunsets. He would sit out on his deck most evenings (in good weather) with his best buddy, Windy, a big blockheaded black lab, and just embrace each sunset with the wonder of the very first. He never tired of the solitude and wonder of the wilderness. They all took turns imparting information about themselves and their take on Mac and Danie's mission until Mark said, "So, how do I fit into this operation?" Mac explained his idea of declaring violent gangs as domestic terrorists and their supporting cartels as terrorists as well. It didn't take Mark long to connect the dots. He never questioned the resolve or integrity of his comrade in arms and signaled his willingness to accommodate the mission in any way he could. As the discussion became more specific regarding the use of a JASOC team engaging the domestic enemy under the full blessing of a new commander-in-chief, Mark felt an excitement long since retired begin to swell within him. His mind began to race, and in short order, he outlined a preliminary operation structure. He offered that he had several retired military professionals who he would like to assemble in the mission planning and execution of the operation should it become a reality. Mac wholeheartedly agreed, and the others, being civilians, listened in utter amazement. It was like being in a great action movie, but this was the real thing with very real people.

"Can a president actually use special forces (SF) teams to combat domestic terrorists within our borders?" Mac asked.

Mark responded by explaining that "'Authority for Use of Military Force to Combat Terrorist Activities Within the United States' is a thirty-seven-page classified United States Department of Justice memorandum dated October twenty-third, 2001. This memo states that the president has both constitutional and statutory authority to use the military as a means to combat terrorist activity within the United States. This memo is a direct result of the terrorist attacks on September eleventh, 2001. Its existence is known because it was referred to in another Department of Justice memo. According to the latter memo, the former memo argued that the Fourth Amendment to the United States Constitution had no application to domestic military operations. The memo has been released to the public.

"This decision was made using a five-part analysis. First, it was found through interpretation by the executive branch of the Constitution that the president of the United States has the authority to 'deploy military force against terrorist threats within the United States.' Second, the enactment of legislation S.J. Resolution Twenty-Three 23, Pub. L. No. 107-40, 115 Stat. 224 (2001) was assessed for legal consequences, and it was determined that the president 'may deploy military force domestically and to prevent and deter similar terrorist attacks.' Third, the Posse Comitatus Act was reviewed, and it was determined that the act only applies to 'domestic use of the armed forces for law enforcement purposed rather than for the performance of military functions.' Fourth, it was determined that military intrusion into terrorist cells does not violate the Fourth Amendment. Fifth and finally, the government has 'a compelling interest in protecting the nation' and 'the war effort would outweigh the relevant privacy interests' in regard to a claim of unreasonable search and seizure. The terrorist attacks that occurred on September 11th, 2001, are unprecedented, and thus, the president's authority to deploy military force against terrorist threats is affirmed. The scale of these terrorist attacks has been viewed as a campaign against the United States and thus viewed as an act of war.

"Members of the First Marine Division were used to control crowds in the 1992 Los Angeles riots. Over the course of the last two hundred and fifteen years, the Army and Marine Corps have been used to intervene in domestic affairs and enforce laws. Federal troops have been used to control riots, protect minorities from violence, break strikes, and guard the borders. Due to the partiality and unreliability of state militias, presidents have found that the use of federal troops was a much more effective means of controlling such domestic disturbances. The use of federal troops in recent times has lessened due to presidents' preference to let state governors utilize state militias to handle issues within the states. Over the last two centuries, laws regarding the use of federal troops to regulate domestic matters have been augmented to reflect lessons learned from previous use of federal troops in civil matters. These laws are based on past experience and were not developed to handle new and unprecedented events such as domestic terrorist attacks.

"So, yes, in my opinion, SF teams can be activated by a sitting president but only after the president clearly identifies the specific aggressor as a domestic terrorist group, but it would be a controversial undertaking at best," Mark explained.

Mac agreed but he contended that considering the marked increase in fear and trepidation inflicted on United States citizens, a compelling legal argument could be made. "Just for argument sake, and in very general terms, how would an SF assault on a gang identified, satisfactorily, as a domestic terrorist group be carried out?" Mac asked his old buddy.

Mark thought for a while, then offered his opinion. He explained that urban warfare within the United States presents a unique circumstance in that the assault group must provide maximum consideration to innocent U.S. citizens. Collateral damage must be kept to an absolute minimum, and zero collateral casualties must be the objective. "The whole picture," he continued, "includes the gangs' members and their weaponry, including intelligence available to them, the proximity to innocent civilians and infrastructure... buildings, roads, etc., and the gang's command and control, cartels located outside the U.S. borders, and embedded operatives—individuals directly controlled by the cartel but not operating directly with the gangs."

"Generally speaking," Mark discussed, "the gang members are relatively untrained thugs who believe that they function as a perceived benefit to themselves but fail to understand that outside forces influence the gangs' activities. There are many factors that may put a young person at higher risk of getting involved in a gang. These might include low self-esteem, feeling hopeless about the future due to a lack of educational and/or financial opportunities, significant unstructured free time outside of school hours, minimal adult supervision, a family history of gang involvement or affiliation, a childhood and/or adolescence in an area with heavy gang activity, no positive role models, and exposure to media that glorifies gang violence, underlying mental health disorders, such as attention-deficit/hyperactivity disorder or depression or alcohol and/or drug use among peers. The reality," he continued, "is that cartels forge unholy alliances with local gangs, merging their malevolence. These unholy pacts amplify criminal activities—drug trafficking, extortion, and turf wars. Gangs, once mere street-level predators, now dance to the cartel's sinister tune.

"The United States intelligence community has extensive information regarding the identification of various cartels, their specific motivation, and their detailed hierarchy, including tracking of senior members and embedded officers. It also possesses technology that far exceeds what is generally known by other than internal members. Without exposing specific details, it can be accepted that identification and real-time tracking are available through satellite and drone surveillance that can provide live imagery, thermal imagery, communications (live and historical location and text), and anticipated combatant ground operations with weapons identification, activation, and payload information.

"Additionally, the military can provide tactical air support in the form of Apache gunships. AH-64A, Apache attack helicopters. (Apache's) are equipped with laser-guided precision Hellfire missiles, seventy-millimeter rockets, and a thirty-millimeter M230 chain gun. In the cockpit, advanced avionics and sighting systems allow the pilots to maneuver track and engage targets in the daytime and at night.

"The Apache has an unconventional two-seat cockpit. Traditionally, two-seat aircraft have the pilot sitting in the front while the weapons system officer sits in the rear. In the Apache, however, the pilot is in the backseat, which is elevated above the front section to provide a better view of the battlespace. The gunner sits up front and controls the weapons and targeting sensor.

"The Apache's targeting sensor is called the Modernized Target Acquisition and Designation Sight, Pilot Night Vision System (M-TADS/PNVS). It is located on the nose of the aircraft and can rotate a hundred and twenty degrees. The M-TADS/PNVS sensor essentially serves as a highly perceptive set of eyes, transmitting real-time imagery of the battlespace to the aviators in high-definition, night vision, or infrared.

"Although protection of innocent civilians precludes massive destructive power such as that which could be called on by utilizing C-130 Gunships (Angel of Death or Angel), the Apache can be utilized for laser precision firepower when the battle moves to more open areas such as fields, parks, or open highways. In these circumstances, the Apache can devastate an enemy force instantly.

"The ground force would likely include undercover operatives embedded among the enemy combatants and specially trained uniformed soldiers who operate as teams and remain in constant communication with each other and operational commanders. These special forces soldiers can be delivered via armored ground vehicles, walk in on foot, or be deployed from Blackhawk helicopters by fast roping down to battle locations.

"The enemy gang members who believe that they are heavily armed and dangerous would face a superior force the likes of which they could never imagine. The engagement would be over so fast that the enemy would be utterly destroyed, and innocent civilians protected.

"Simultaneously, the gang command and control locations of cartel headquarters located outside the U.S. would be disseminated by a barrage of rocket and missile fire delivered from fighter aircraft, bombers, Angles, and offshore naval vessels. In addition to the total destruction of enemy command and control locations, individual enemy operatives would be eliminated by surgical ground or air assaults regardless of where they are located.

"After such an attack, the United States would broadcast details of the battle and warn, in no uncertain terms, that all other cartel and gang activities have a forty-eight-hour window to cease and desist or face a similar fate."

Mark concluded by offering that such an assault would require close support from members of the intelligence community (domestic and global), input from vetted political experts (domestic and political), and several U.S. agencies, including but not limited to the CIA, FBI, DEA, ICE, CIS, NSC, and state and local law enforcement agencies. "No small task," he added.

"When and if this hypothetical action comes to fruition, I'd be proud to provide whatever assistance I can," he said, and with that, the gang drifted off to a myriad of less intense discussions while they enjoyed the magnificent sunset from his deck.

# CHAPTER 15
## HEADED TO VIRGINIA

The next morning was another beautiful Montana day. Mac, usually the first to be up and around, found Mark already sitting out on the deck with a coffee and Windy. Mark hadn't slept much because he couldn't shut his mind down. He confided to Mac that he had opted to retire in the mountains for its peace and beauty but also because he needed a place to avoid the rat race that he considered living among the general population. He admitted that the decades of service and the traumatic effect that his many missions had taken on his soul were no small thing, but he affirmed that, after long and hard consideration, he was ready and willing to accept the mission should it materialize. He said that he felt it was time to take dramatic action to set things back on a course that was more aligned with what he considered normalcy.

Mac explained that the team would be splitting up with Jim, Katie, and Pete returning home, and he and Danie headed to Virginia to meet with Mason Dewitt to discuss the campaign finance structure. Mac had already coordinated with his friend and arranged to meet him at his Virginia horse ranch.

Mark said that the weather was great for the flight and that once the rest were up, fed, and packed, he'd fly everyone to Helena, where Stan was waiting with the jet to ferry the team to their respective destinations.

Danie was the next to make an appearance, followed shortly by the rest. Mac took over the chef duties and presented a breakfast fit for a king. The group dined and continued discussing the bizarre nature of the mission, with Danie continually dodging the understandable questions about her origin and details about the future. Everyone knew and agreed she was limited to what she could disclose but the temptation was irresistible, and the questions usually met with her wonderful smile and a chuckle.

They all ate, and by 0900, Mark lifted off with the gang and headed for Helena. They landed after the half-hour ride, and Stan was waiting at the fixed base operations (FBO) building. Before parting, Mark assured Mac that he would get to work looking into his end of the mission and that he would keep him updated on his progress.

The jet was airborne withing a half hour and headed for the first stop in Rockland, Maine. At more than five hundred nautical miles per hour (KTS), it would be about a five-hour flight, and the jet wouldn't require a refueling stop enroute. Pete offered the team the chance to stay at his place overnight to rest up and all agreed.

The discussion about the mission continued throughout the flight, and Jim said that he would begin assembling a small political affairs team of his own to ensure that Mac got on the 2024 ballot as planned.

Mac, of course, made arrangements for substantial funding to be managed by Jim for his team's requirements.

Pete offered that he would also assemble a small team of IT experts and start developing a plan to get Mac and his mission exposed to the public. He suggested that an online platform with a phone app that was user-friendly, free, and capable of collecting users' input to be tabulated and analyzed. He continued by explaining that besides the actual software development, he would need to recruit a small team of psychologists with expertise in social media and gaming and graphic artists to develop the look and feel that is needed to draw the attention of the public and keep them wanting more. "It won't be cheap," he cautioned, but Mac said that he has the resources and money should not be a deciding factor.

Stan made another perfect landing in Rockland shortly after 0400 Eastern Standard Time (EST), and while Stan tended to the jet, the rest drove over to Pete's place once again. Everyone was pretty worn out from the trip, even though the jet was as comfortable as any living room. They had a light meal on the deck, and all turned in early.

In the morning, it was overcast and windy, so they had breakfast inside, and then Pete drove Mac, Danie, Jake, and Katie to the airport, where Stan was ready and waiting for the run to Virginia. The weather was fair in Rockland but just above the minimums (the required ceiling and visibility for a landing) in Virginia. Due to the weather conditions, Stan filed a flight plan to Richmond Executive-Chesterfield County Airport with instrument approaches that allowed Stan to arrive with minimum conditions. Mason had been contacted and agreed to pick up Mac and Danie at the airport, which was about an hour's drive from his ranch, which was northeast of Lynchburg.

The flight was smooth above the clouds at twenty-four thousand feet, and Mac flew right seat (co-pilot) while Danie relaxed in the luxurious cabin. The hour-and-a-half flight went by quickly, and Stan made yet another textbook instrument approach and landing. It had gotten a little rough on approach due to the weather, but Stan and Mac's jet had no problem handling it.

Mason was waiting at the FBO, and Stan stayed at a nearby hotel while Mason, Mac, and Danie drove out to the ranch. Mason was a single guy; he lost his wife to cancer many years ago. He had no children and since retiring, he devoted most of his time to his horses and occasional fly-fishing trips. He is an unassuming man, the kind of guy who doesn't stand out in a crowd, but when he speaks, his voice and vocabulary command immediate attention. Having served as finance director for a previous successful Democrat presidential candidate, he was the perfect fit to oversee Mac's campaign financial strategy.

Mason's ranch was a sprawling fifty-acre spread with manicured grounds and impressive white fencing. The three arrived at his house and after Mac and Danie got settled in their room, they all assembled on Mason's second-story porch that overlooked the fenced pastures with horses wandering about. "So, I've heard the Cliff Notes, Mac, what's the real story here?" Mason asked his old friend. Mac and Danie once again went through their story, and Danie's part of the mission caused

Mason to pause. She was a very convincing orator, and after a couple of drinks and another hour of questions and answers, Mason said, "I've known you and Jim for a long time, Mac, and if you guys are in, then I guess I'll pitch in as well."

He went on to explain that in a presidential campaign, well-structured and clearly presented accounting is critical. He continued to say that Mac's finances, before the recent windfall, were straightforward and would easily withstand the intense scrutiny that would be encountered. His selection of well-known and reputable accounting and legal firms was a great start. Mac and Danie's personal background would be tied directly to any financial review, and he asked how Danie would be explained. Danie made a new announcement that she hadn't presented until now. She told the two men that a past had been created by her mission partners from her time. She possessed a valid passport, driver's license, and other pertinent documentation. According to her documentation, she was born in Maine, and attended local schools, including a degree from the University of Maine at Orono in business management. She was never married and inherited a substantial portfolio from her father. Her history was flawless and would withstand the intense scrutiny that comes with a presidential run.

Mason acknowledged her input and suggested that he assemble a small team to oversee the management of Mac's campaign finances. Mac agreed and told his old friend that he would make arrangements for Mason to meet with his accounting firm and his legal team immediately.

It was a long evening, with banter about Mac and Danie's plan continuing well into the evening. Around midnight, they all decided to call it a night and retired to their respective sleeping quarters.

As they climbed into bed Danie suggested that, with the team assembled and financing in place, perhaps a break was in order while the respective sub-teams got organized. It was only mid-summer, and they had another year or so until the election. Mac ran his fingers through her soft black hair and fixed his eyes on hers. Danie made him feel relaxed and excited at the same time. It was unlike any experience he could recall. "Sure," he said. The fact was that, even though things were going perfectly so far, he was emotionally fatigued. He recalled the relief he felt when he first paddled onto the lake before he met Danie. The whole point of his trip was to wrestle with his frustration with the current state of affairs in the country. In the wild, things made sense to Mac. They always did. He longed to be refreshed by the wilderness again. That was it.

Mac asked Danie how she felt about spending a couple of weeks on another remote lake in Maine. She smiled and told him that it sounded perfect to her. Mac went on to describe Chemquasabamticook Lake to her. It was another lake with only slightly more access than Allagash Lake, where the adventure began. He told her that they would take the jet to Presque Isle, Maine, and swap to a Cessna 180 on floats. Mac was current with this aircraft and said that he would fly them the eighty miles southwest of Presque Isle, and they would set up camp on a little peninsula on the western shore. There was no vehicle access to the spot, and although it was lowlands, the shore on the point was rocky, with a magnificent little white sand beach in a cove just to the north. He warned her that there would be no shortage of mosquitoes and black flies, but good fly dope (bug spray) and a large, screened tent would make life more pleasant. They would tie a sixteen-foot, square stern (the back of the canoe was squared to accommodate a small motor) on the floats that would provide transportation around the lake.

They agreed and drifted off into the most restful sleep that either had experienced since Allagash Lake.

In the morning, Danie and Mason found Mac outside, on the deck, with a coffee. "Still an early riser?" Mason asked his buddy. Mac said that old habits die hard, and Mason followed by telling him that he was in for a whole new set of experiences with this latest mission.

"No question about that!" Mac replied as he poured a coffee for Mason and Danie.

Mac filled Mason in on his decision to take a break, up in Maine, for a week or so, and Mason agreed that it was a great idea but suggested that Mac keep his SAT phone (a portable phone that used satellites and didn't require any cell service) to keep a handle on the progress from the respective teams. "Already figure on that," Mac replied.

They all spent the following few days just relaxing and doing a little horseback riding. Danie was excited to ride because she had never been on a horse. Mac, on the other hand, was quite comfortable on horseback because, while he was posted in Montana with Customs and Border

Protection (CBP), he was lucky enough to do quite a bit of riding with a buddy, Bill (a fellow officer we'll call Bill) who owned a nice ranch near the port crossing between Canada and the United States.

Once Bill had become satisfied that Mac was reasonably competent in the saddle, they often rode out on the prairie along the old Lewis and Clark route. Bill was a Montana resident, and he seemed to know all about the history of the old days. Some nights, they would camp at spots where the early Indians had made their camps. Around the fire in the evening Bill would recount stories passed down to him from his grandfather, Jimbo. He would talk about the Assiniboine Tribe that his great-grandfather had close relations with. The entire Assiniboine Tribe, including females, were known as excellent bison hunters, horse riders, and fighters.

Like many Native American Tribes that first lived in Montana, they were known for trading pemican—an exquisite dish made from preserved bison meat and wild berries—for firearms delivered by traders on the upper Missouri River.

Bill's great-grandfather had settled by the Missouri River in 1870 and enjoyed a wonderful relationship with the Assiniboins despite the ongoing Indian wars. Montana was a sparsely settled region at that time, and Jimbo ran a small cattle ranch and had to drive his herd down to Wyoming until the railroad came through in 1884. He avoided making the trip to Wolf Point except to buy supplies and sell cattle after the railroad came through. Consequently, he was viewed as a non-threat by the Assiniboins.

Bill's stories provided Mac with a more open perspective of the early days in our country. He explained, based on stories passed directly through his family, that the modern impression that the native people were strictly wholesome lovers of nature was incorrect. They were just people. They had the same strengths and flaws that any people have. They were just a different culture. The many tribes, as nature has created us, held different values and could be violent as well as caring. "Just people," he used to say. Mac treasured the many wonderful opportunities that he had been presented throughout his life and wished that more people had the chance to view life from a more informed perspective.

# CHAPTER 16
## BACK TO MAINE

Their stay with Mason ended with a ride back to the jet that Stan had fueled and readied for the trip back to Maine. They lifted off on the morning of the third day with Mac in the left seat (getting some training from Stan) and Danie relaxing in the cabin. They touched down in Presque Isle in the early afternoon, and Mac and Danie drove over to the local Hampton Inn for a few days of preparing for their next adventure.

The following morning Mac met Stan at the airport, and they drove over to Hanson Lake (a small pond just off the northwest end of the airport). Stan had arranged to have a Cessna 185 Skywagon on floats docked and ready to give Mac a few hours of refresher training. The C-185 is a high-wing single-engine aircraft equipped with a 300 hp (224 kW) Continental IO-520-D engine that provides plenty of power for float operations carrying significant cargo. Mac and Danie planned to bring plenty of creature comforts for their vacation.

It had been a couple of years since Mac had piloted a float plane, and although he was technically still current, he opted to get a refresher from his old instructor pilot. Mac fired up the powerful engine, performed all of the pre-flight checklist, and they moved away from the dock slowly. The wind was twelve nautical miles per hour (KTS) from the north, so they planned to taxi on the step, a maneuver with moderate power that allowed the plane to rise slightly out of the water and only maintain minimal contact with the south end of the pond. Mac hadn't lost his touch, and the taxi was flawless. Approaching the south end, Mac throttled back (reduced the power), and the plane settled into the water for a slow turn into the wind. A pilot always takes off as closely into the wind as possible to allow more air to flow over the wing, creating lift as possible. Once Mac was established on a heading directly into the light wind, he set two clicks or about twenty degrees of flaps, powered up (increased power), bringing the prop (setting for the angle of the propeller) and throttle (control of the power) to 100 percent and held back slightly on the yolk (The pilot uses the yoke to control the attitude of the plane, usually in both pitch and roll. Rotating the control wheel controls the ailerons and the roll axis). The plane roared to life and gently lifted onto the step, where less friction with the water allowed it to gain speed faster. Mac rotated (reached an appropriate speed for takeoff) nicely, and the old workhorse started climbing into the morning sky. Once airborne, Mac reduced the prop and throttle to about 2,700 RPM (squared the prop and throttle) and reduced the flaps to zero for less drag and more efficient flight operations.

He had set in a location for Chemquasabamticook Lake on his GPS navigational instrument, and he eased west to a heading that put him on course for the lake. He thought about how much easier navigation had become with the introduction of GPS. In the early days, he would have relied on a radial emitted by a VOR, a (VOR stands for very high-frequency omnidirectional range and is a navigation aid (navaid). At the most simple level, a VOR is a type of navigation system for aircraft, using very high frequency radio signals emitted by radio beacons. And his maps utilizing dead reckoning. Dead reckoning is one step up from pilotage; it adds another level of formality. With dead reckoning, a pilot has a little help finding objects in low visibility or when they can't see from one landmark to the next. Dead reckoning also involves a little bit of math. By figuring out the plane's speed and course over the ground, the pilot can determine where they are based on how long they've been flying. Or in other words, they'll know where they'll be in fifteen minutes, thirty minutes, or an hour. This extra work has even more benefits, though. If a pilot knows how long each leg of the flight takes, then they know how long the entire trip will take. And that means they can complete the most important thing of all–fuel planning. Dead reckoning answers questions like, how long will it take to get to my destination and how much fuel will I use to get there? But today, he simply had to input a location into his GPS and follow the indicator. All good bush pilots always prepare and have available the older methods in case of a GPS failure. Many modern pilots have gotten into serious situations by relying too heavily on new equipment and disregarding general pilotage (Pilotage is the practice of spotting landmarks and checkpoints on the ground and corroborating them with a map while flying. Pilotage is a complex skill that requires pilots to learn their routes, memorize important checkpoints, and memorize the distance of checkpoints at different altitudes.

The short half-hour ride at 140 KTS (160 MPH) was pleasant and routine. The wind was still out of the north, so Mac set up his final approach to the northeast/southwest lake from the south. He descended to 1,500 feet above ground level (AGL) and reduced the power to 1,800 RPM (70% power). He dropped in twenty degrees of flaps (two clicks in the skywagon) and established an approach speed of eighty KTS. He approached the lake along the southwest shoreline to provide better altitude perception and eased toward the water. As the plane was just a few feet above the water, he backed off the throttle and glided to a perfect water landing.

He and Stan made several takeoffs and landings, then they headed back to Presque Isle. After landing and docking at Hanson Lake, Mac headed to the hotel to meet Danie. It was getting close to noon, and the couple had lunch and returned to the room to start planning the gear for their trip. Besides the plane and the canoe, Mac wanted to bring a small 5HP gasoline motor for the boat. Unlike the basic camping tents that they both used on Allagash Lake, they decided to take a larger geodesic tent equipped with a covered and screened vestibule for meals without the attention of the ferocious black flies and mosquitoes. They decided on a nice menu since they had plenty of room for cargo in the powerful skywagon!

They decided to fly out the following morning because the weather was forecast to be clear with a slight northeast wind that was perfect for an approach to Chemquasabamticook Lake. They spent the rest of the day with Stan loading the plane. The canoe had to be secured properly on the starboard (right) float and the gear arranged so that the weight was distributed evenly. Their cargo weighed in at around 600 lbs. (well within the capacity of the beefy plane). Stan had removed the passenger seats to allow for easier loading and unloading of cargo.

Work was completed by early afternoon, and the three decided to have the evening meal together. Mac and Stan had known each other since the early eighties when they were both assigned to Loring AFB in Limestone, Maine. Ten years Mac's junior, Stan was a cross-trainee (transferred from a different job) to air traffic control and already a commercial pilot with his instructor certification. Mac, at the time, was a private pilot. He had trained in England while assigned there for three years. Stan had taken Mac under his wing as a pilot and trained him to earn his complex (high-performance aircraft), seaplane, and multi-engine ratings.

Stan and his wife had divorced in the late eighties, and he, sadly, lost his next wife to cancer fifteen years later. After that he remained single and continued flying commercially until a few years before Mac contacted him for the mission. Stan was one of those freaks of nature physically. At sixty-five, he was in better shape than most men at forty. He accepted the offer to pilot Mac's planes until the mission was ended one way or another.

During the meal, among the stories floated by the two buddies, Stan began to recount his favorite "Mac Air Traffic Control (ATC) tale."

It was the dead of winter in 1986 at Loring Air Force Base, Maine. Stan was the Watch Supervisor in the Tower, and Mac was the Senior Controller (Watch Supervisor) who also worked for the boards due to reduced manning) —in the Radar Approach Control (RAPCON) facility. It was a swing shift (1600 to 2300), and there was no traffic due to a blizzard. Nearly two feet of heavy snow had already fallen, and the conditions were indefinite ceiling zero, visibility zero, snow (WOXOS) with winds gusting to forty KTS. The guys were just hanging around, playing cards to kill time. At about 2000, a call came in from Boston Control Center (BOS) informing Mac that a flight of five A7s, The LTV A-7 Corsair II is an American carrier-capable subsonic light attack aircraft designed and manufactured by Ling-Temco-Vought (LTV). The A-7 was developed during the early 1960s as a replacement for the Douglas A-4 Skyhawk.)

They were diverting to Navy Brunswick, Maine (Naval Air Station Brunswick (IATA: NHZ, ICAO: KNHZ, FAA LID: NHZ), also known as NAS Brunswick or the Brunswick Naval Air Station, was a military airport located 2 miles (3.2 km) southeast of Brunswick, Maine, with a number of navy-operated maritime patrol aircraft from their original destination due to flight conditions. They were going to attempt a Precision Approach Radar (PAR) (Precision approach radar or PAR is a type of radar guidance system designed to provide lateral and vertical guidance to an aircraft pilot for landing until the landing threshold is reached. Controllers monitoring the PAR displays observe each aircraft's position and issue instructions to the pilot that keep the aircraft on course and glide path during the final approach. After the aircraft reaches the decision height (DH) or decision altitude (DA), further guidance is advisory only. The overall concept is known as the ground-controlled approach (GCA), and this name was also used to refer to the radar systems in the early days of its development, but the weather at NAS was deteriorating, and their last attempt would be Loring if they missed their approach. If they made the final diversion to Loring, they would be flying on fumes (almost out of fuel with absolutely no room for error).

Mac instructed the PAR controller to double-check the system to be certain that everything was perfect in case the A7s made the run to Loring. No sooner had the PAR controller assured Mac that everything was good. Boston called and informed Mac that the A7s had missed at NAS and were enroute to Loring. Airfield operations were furiously working to keep the runway open, but it was a nearly impossible effort. Then the call came in, "Loring Approach, Spong 01 (flight leader), flight of five A7s, bingo fuel (emergency fuel situation) inbound from Navy Brunswick for PAR approach." Mac, who was working as Approach Control, answered and provided the airport information and weather conditions.

"Approach were sucking fumes, and I'll accept less than minimum separation (FAA required three miles or one thousand feet of separation). I've got to get my boys on the ground and can't afford a miss." Mac had three controllers on duty and needed one to vector the A7s to the final course and planned to use two to run the PARs. He decided to work final (the PARs with another controller. His other final controller objected to providing less than minimum separation, but Mac ordered him to comply, and he agreed. They decided to maintain about two miles of separation on the final. Mac told the lead that he would agree to his request but cautioned that the runway was buried, and they would have zero visibility after touchdown. The lead ordered his pilots to immediately turn off the runway into the snow as soon as they slowed sufficiently. They would alternatively turn off to the right and then the left with each successive landing. Command Post (Operates and monitors voice, data, and alerting systems. Develops, maintains, and initiates quick reaction checklists supporting situations such as suspected or actual sabotage, nuclear incidents, natural disasters, aircraft accidents or incidents, evacuations, dispersal, and aerospace anomalies. Maintains operational status displays. Maintains proficiency in Theater Battle Management Core Systems (TBMCS) and aircraft flight following systems. Establishes staffing, communications, and facility requirements.) heard the conversation between Mac and the lead aircraft and instructed Mac, on direct order from the wing commander, to maintain minimum FAA separation standards. Mac responded that if he did, they were going to lose aircraft and pilots and refused. Now the shit show started! Mac's other final controller refused to run the approaches with less than minimum separation. Mac was lost until Stan called down from the tower and told Mac that he was leaving the tower with two controllers and coming down to run finals with Mac. Calls were coming in from the Command Post and air traffic control managers ordering Mac to comply with the wing commander, but he refused. The aircraft was now only forty miles out, and Stan arrived at the RAPCON door. "Are you sure about this shit?" Mac asked his buddy, and Stan just nodded and said, "Fuck it, these guys need us." Both of their air traffic control careers were about to be finished.

Mac accepted the first A7 with the words, "Spong zero three, Loring final controller, ten miles from final, do not acknowledge further transmissions..." And so, it began. Each aircraft was instructed with the correct direction to make as soon as possible after touchdown. The first A7 never saw the runway lights until Mac called, "Over landing threshold, contact tower point seven after landing.". The pilot felt the wheels touch as he caught sight of the runway in a blur of blowing snow. He cranked the aircraft to his starboard (right) and plowed into the snow to a safe landing. It was the same for each successive plane. No one, no controller or pilot, had ever witnessed anything like this before. Before the last plane touched down, there were loud knocks on the RAPCON door, and Mac ordered the approach controller to ignore the knocks and shouts.

"We're all down and safe approach! Great fucking work!" the lead pilot called to Mac.

"Great, I'm about to be arrested for disobeying direct orders, but I'd do it again any time, Sir," Mac responded.

"Are you shitting me? I'm headed into base operations now, and we'll damn well see about that!" Spong zero one came back. The pilots exited their aircraft and had to walk through the deep, howling snow because operations couldn't get a vehicle out to them.

Now Mac opened the door to the RAPCON. He was looking at military police, his squadron commander (a major with no FAA rating), the RAPCON chief controller, who immediately relieved Mac of his position and assumed control of the facility, and the tower chief, who relieved Stan of his position. Both men were placed under arrest, and as they began to leave the facility, Navy Captain (we'll call him Jim Smith came storming down the stairs still in his flight suit, covered in snow. "What the fuck is going on here?" he screamed.

"Sir, these men have been relieved of duty for disobeying direct orders and violating FAA safety regulations," said the squadron commander.

"The fuck they are," Captain Smith barked. "Wake up the Wing Commander and get his ass down here, and I mean right now! He and I will sort this shit out. My men are safe, and three of us ran out of fuel on the taxi!" He asked who was the RAPCON watch supervisor and Mac was pointed out. The squadron commander started babbling something, and Captain Smith barked, "You shut the fuck up!" He walked over to Mac and said, "That was the greatest air traffic control I've ever seen. Thank you, Sir! (Officers never addressed enlisted men as sir, which showed the utmost respect. It was an unbelievable situation.

"Sir, the Wing Commander is on the radio for you," one of the command post officers who were also present offered.

Captain Smith took the radio. "Sir, I can't get to the RAPCON because of the road conditions."

The wing commander said, "Okay, Sergeant McNamara just saved five Navy pilots, and you have him arrested. You and I need to talk! I don't care if you have to summon God himself; you get the officers club opened and meet us there, and I mean now!" Nobody screwed with a decorated Navy captain pilot.

"It'll be done, sir," came the rather meek response from the wing commander. The rest of the people were in shock.

"Get us some transport and everyone, and I mean everyone, with me to the club!"

It took some time, but eventually, a couple of heavy-duty snow vehicles arrived at the door of base operations, and the group boarded for the quick ride to the club. When they arrived, they were met by the wing commander and a couple of men to man the bar. A wing commander is God on his base, but Captain Smith's reputation preceded him, and everything calmed down quickly. With the pouring of the first drink, Captain Smith raised a glass and said, "To Mac and Stan, the most goddamned air traffic controller I've ever had the pleasure to meet!" Everyone raised their glasses and cheered as well. I think the wing commander and the squadron commander were choking on theirs. Both Mac and Stan received decorations for their efforts.

# CHAPTER 17
## CHEMQUASABAMTICOOK LAKE

Mac and Danie had an early breakfast in town and arrived at Hanson Lake at about 0800. Stan was already on the plane, double-checking all the cargo and the aircraft itself. Mac performed his own pre-flight inspection (a complete check of the aircraft that must be performed by the pilot himself). Everything checked out satisfactorily, and Stan bid the two good days and wished them a nice trip.

The powerful engine roared to life, and Mac taxied slowly away from the dock. The wind was, again, out of the northeast at eight KTS, so he taxied to the southwest end of the lake and turned into the wind. He performed his final checklist and eased the throttle to full power, holding gentle back pressure on the yolk until he felt the plane rise onto the step. Now, he eased back on the yolk as the aircraft gained speed. At Vr ($V_R$ is the speed at which the pilot gently pulls back on the control column to lift the nose off the runway during takeoff, Mac eased back on the yolk, and the skywagon left the water and embraced flight.

It was a nice half-hour flight to the lake. Danie never tired of flying, it was a surreal experience for her. Mac lined up from the southwestern end of the lake and established a final approach course close to the shoreline. The wind was only five KTS, and making a water landing close to shore provided a better depth perception than landing in the middle of the lake. He touched down short of the landing beach and cut one magneto (An aircraft magneto is an engine-driven electrical generator that uses permanent magnets and coils to produce high voltage to fire the aircraft. Spark plugs; magnetos are used in piston aircraft engines and are known for their simplicity and reliability) and slowly approached the sandy beach. He cut the power completely close to shore and drifted in until the Edo 3430 floats touched the sand. Mac got out first and secured the aircraft to a tree near the beach.

It was a beautiful morning, and they had all the time in the world to unpack the gear. Mac removed the canoe first and stowed it on the beach, then they brought out the large tent and set it upright on a flat part of the beach about fifty feet from the water. Getting the tent and vestibule up and screened meant protection from the ferocious black flies and mosquitoes they were bound to deal with. One might wonder why they would even consider choosing a place where insects were such an issue, but you would have to experience the wonder of such a location to fully embrace that decision. It was hot, and that kept the insect issue to a minimum during the daytime.

By late afternoon, all the gear was stowed, their two-person cot and light sleeping bag were set up inside the tent, and Mac had put in enough dry firewood for the first few days. They sprayed the inside of the tent, so as evening approached, they were quite protected from the menacing bugs.

It cooled nicely at sunset, and Mac built a small fire just outside the vestibule for them to sit by and watch and listen as evening morphed into nighttime. True to its name, the loon's eerie call ushered in the night. Mac couldn't have been more relaxed and Danie told him, once more, that this was much more beautiful than she was prepared for.

Over some chilled wine (Mac packed a solar-powered cooler), they sat together, saying very little and just took in the simplicity and peace. It wasn't long before they decided to call it a night and retired.

Danie woke up the next morning to the sound of the loons. It was just after daybreak and Mac already had the breakfast fire going with coffee brewing. It was still cool outside, and the insects were pleasantly absent. Mac turned to his breathtaking partner and, holding a small box, said, "What's this?"

Danie was physically shaken because the box had an image from her time on it. "I don't know," she answered. She asked him where he got it, and he told her that it was just sitting on the sand right in front of the plane. Danie suggested that it was sent from her time, but she failed to understand how they would have known specifically where to leave it. She took her seat by the fire and Mac handed her the box, unopened. She anxiously opened it, and inside was a letter and a flash drive.

The letter explained that they felt that the contents of the drive would prove helpful to Mac's IT team and nothing more. Danie said she was completely unaware that they would ever receive such information but suggested that it was likely important to the mission.

Mac thought he had come to grips with the whole concept of the mission, but this tossed his poor head back into a whirlwind of confusion. He asked her if they should cut the vacation short and get the drive to the team, but Danie suggested they leave the camp set up and fly the drive back to Presque Isle, read the contents, and then decide the next course of action. Mac agreed, and after their coffee, they fired up the 185 and headed to Presque Isle.

Once airborne and within cell reception, Mac called Stan. He explained what had transpired and asked his friend to meet them at the Hanson Lake dock. Stan, of course, agreed and was waiting when they docked.

They drove straight to Stan's hotel and opened the drive on his computer. The anxiety was so thick you could cut it with a knife. Mac was at the keyboard and the drive held an explanation and several attachments. The note said that their IT folks had provided some algorithms and schematics for simple hardware that would significantly aid in providing live feedback from the voting populace.

Mac contacted Pete and arranged to forward the content of the drive to him. Pete asked Mac to remain at the computer until he received the data and was certain that he could open the contents. Mac, of course, agreed and sent the contents. Pete quickly responded that he received the email and asked Mac to standby. The contents of the attachments were beyond Mac's understanding, and he couldn't wait to hear if Pete could make sense of them.

The next half hour seemed like an eternity to the three anxious friends, but then the phone call came in. Mac put Pete on speaker, and his voice was audibly excited. Pete explained that he was able to open the attachments and that they provided a schematic for an app (Apps are a significant part of the technology-driven world we live in and can enhance a person's life, enjoyment, and productivity. Apps are also regularly used by companies, both large and small, to streamline production and increase ease of work. In this article, we discuss what an app is, the different types of apps, and examples of common apps used today.) and a piece of hardware to receive real-time data from the users and compile it in a manner that would provide remarkable drill-down reports (A drill-down report provides a more granular view of data by assuming a hierarchical relationship between different data levels. It allows users to access more detailed data overviews from a single, comprehensive view. In a drill-down report, users can click on specific elements to explore multidimensional data without switching between visualizations1. For example, imagine you have a graph showing website traffic sources. With a drill-down report, you could further break down the traffic from social media into platforms like Facebook, Instagram, TikTok, and Pinterest. Similarly, if you have a list of customers by country, a drill-down report would allow you to access a more detailed overview of customers by city with just one click. These reports enhance decision-making by providing deeper insights into data and helping identify trends and patterns. Pete said that this software and hardware information would revolutionize interaction with the entire nation for the team.

Pete told Mac that he would get with his team, as well as Jim and Mason's teams, and report back in a week or two. Mac thanked him, and that was that.

The three decided to have breakfast with cocktails since they were all operating on high power and needed to calm down a little. Mac arranged for a room for the night, and Mac called the airfield and ordered to have the 185 refueled and ready for departure in the morning.

It was already close to noon, so they elected for brunch and the much-needed cocktails. At brunch, Mac confessed, again, that he felt like he was in over his head with this mission, but Danie countered by assuring him that although it seemed too much to handle, it would all work out. There was always something about her that was able to calm the situation and bring a sense of believability to the impossible. The three gradually relaxed, and the drinks flowed. The mood morphed from high anxiety to a celebratory sort of jubilation. Mac and Danie decided to have an early evening and fly back to Chemquasabamticook Lake in the morning.

The three friends met again for breakfast, and then Stan drove them back to the plane. Mac repeated his earlier performance, and in short order, they were airborne and enroute back to camp. Again, Mac settled the skywagon onto the lake and docked with the rear end secured just touching the sandy beach.

It was an overcast day with cloud ceilings at about 4,500 feet which had allowed Mac to fly VFR below the overcast all the way to the lake.

They checked the campsite, and all was exactly as they had left it. Danie asked her new friend what he would like to do. Mac was quick to respond that the overcast day with light wind offered a perfect opportunity to hit the lake in the canoe. He offered to show Danie some great spots around the lake and do some trolling with a downrigger (Downriggers are devices used while trolling to keep a bait or lure at the desired depth. In practice, fish swim at different depths according to factors such as the temperature and amount of light in the water, and the speed and direction of water currents. A downrigger consists of a short horizontal pole that supports a weight, typically about four pounds of lead, on a steel cable. A clip called a "line release" attaches the fishing line to the weight, and the bait or lure is attached to the release at the same time.

Danie was more than happy to hit the lake as suggested. Mac attached the small outboard motor to the rear of the canoe. They packed some fresh water, sandwiches, and some wine and shoved off for some relaxation. Once they were in deep enough water, Mac set up the downrigger and lowered his grey ghost streamer to fifty feet. Salmon and brook trout prefer cooler water, and at this time of year, the fifty-degree ideal temperature was around fifty feet. No sooner had they set the line and began fishing in earnest than Danie spotted an osprey circling above. As she watched, the beautiful 'fish hawk' made a dive into the water and emerged with its breakfast flapping from its razor-sharp talons. "Pretty cool, eh?" Mac asked her. "Everything out here is magnificent," he explained once again, and she couldn't agree more. Mac had the rod holder set up in front so Danie could handle the fish if they were fortunate enough to hook up. They rode for about a half hour when the line snapped tight, and the rod began to bounce wildly. "Fish on," Mac shouted, and Danie grabbed the rod and reel and began to fight her first fish. "Good fish!" he said, "Don't horse him. Let him run if he wants to." The fish made several hard runs then it became a series of shorter wild turns and pulls. Soon, the water exploded as a silvery landlocked salmon made the first of many spectacular jumps. These fish are known for their aerial displays and are highly sought-after sport fish.

Finally, the beautiful salmon made another leap with its head thrashing, and the hook pulled free. "I lost it!" she said in utter disappointment.

"No worries. The fun is the fight, and you got that in spades," Mac said. He was right; it was exciting, and she wouldn't soon forget her first salmon.

They trolled another half hour with no luck, so Mac hauled in the fishing gear and headed for a spot on the western edge of the lake where a nice spring fed the lake. They landed the canoe, and Mac filled a three-gallon cooler with fresh, sweet water for camp drinking. The spring was only about fifteen minutes by canoe from camp and would serve as their source of drinking water for the duration of the trip.

They landed back at camp in time to get the fire going before the evening transformation to nighttime. Sitting by the fire that evening, they shared thoughts about the nature of people in general and how people seem to have always behaved in a manner contrary to nature. As a species, humans, from the beginning, have been the most vicious, self-serving creatures on the planet.

Having acknowledged human distinct differences from other species, Danie commented on the polar differences of many people. Folks who embrace the intrinsic value of family and close societal contacts. Their inherent disapproval of unnecessary violence and injustice. Mac agreed and continued that it was the very fact that most people are inherently solid, gentle creatures that encouraged him to accept Danie's mission. "Sure," he said, "there's a lot of evil in the world but it's getting worse these days, driven by deliberate behavior modification introduced by social media that includes what we have come to consider news outlets." They agreed that righting the figurative ship, if possible, was a mission worth undertaking.

They spent another twelve days basking in the serenity that is the wilderness and finally decided to pack up camp and return to the mission. Of course, the day that they decided to leave, it rained with low ceilings and visibility, so their return was delayed for two days.

On the last evening in camp, Mac asked Danie if she would consider becoming his wife, and she agreed without hesitation. Mac wondered if her new identity would withstand the scrutiny of the background checks and media digging that accompanies the spouse of a potential presidential candidate, and she assured him that it most certainly would. That was good enough for him, and they entered a whole new dimension of their relationship.

The following morning brought clear skies and a gentle south wind. They packed up the 185 and left the balanced calm of the lake to embrace whatever was to be their fate in the months and years to come.

# CHAPTER 18
## BACK TO PRESQUE ISLE AND BEYOND

They arrived back in Presque Isle around noontime. Stan met them at the dock and helped Mac unload the plane. While they were unloading, Mac asked Stan to get the jet ready to fly back to Nebraska the following morning, and Stan, of course, agreed.

They finished in the late afternoon, and the three had an evening meal together. At supper, Mac informed Stan that he and Danie planned to marry, and the suds flowed for real. Over the course of the evening, Mac suggested that he and Danie should find a better place to live than his little apartment in Lincoln. He could afford almost anything that they wanted, but neither wanted to appear too flamboyant. Stan figures that a nice place on the ocean with good high-speed Internet might be just the ticket. Mac and Danie agreed, and Mac reached out to one of his daughters, who was a very successful real estate agent in southern Maine. They were still at the restaurant when Mac's daughter Kate called back. She was excited to help her dad and said she was aware of a beautiful home in Rockland that was situated on twelve acres of land with nearly a quarter mile of beachfront. Mac told Stan to scrap the trip to Nebraska and plan a run to Rockland in the morning. Stan asked him if he wanted to wait an hour for the next change of plans, and they all broke into hardy laughter.

In the morning, they all boarded the jet, and although the weather was less than optimum, Stan had no problem ushering the aircraft to a perfect landing in Rockland less than twenty minutes after takeoff. Pete had offered to have Mac, Danie, Stan, and Kate all stay with him for a couple of days because he wanted to pursue more detailed discussions about the new technology that Danie's people had made available to the team.

Pete met the gang at the airport, and they drove to his place, with Kate following in her own vehicle. At Pete's house Mac was surprised to see Jake waiting. With introductions accomplished and everyone settled into their respective rooms, they all joined in the living room as it was too miserable outside to talk. Most of the details were new to Kate, and, to say the least, she was dizzy with information overload. Kate was a tall, beautiful young lady, and most of Mac's close friends all joked that he couldn't possibly be responsible for such a lovely and accomplished woman.

Pete took the lead initially. He explained that he felt it was imperative to have Jake at this meeting because the new technology was going to jump-start the process, and they needed his expertise regarding the politically correct way to initiate Mac's introduction. He continued to explain that the software code and the hardware interface, although completely compatible with existing technology, were remarkably advanced. The idea, he said, was to be able to reach as many potential voters as possible and be able to receive real time responses from them. In short, the team would be able to provide information completely free from any other media source and receive live input that would be processed and tabulated almost immediately. This capability would effectively eliminate the need to consider the typical polling numbers that consume other candidates. Additionally, there was a development that afforded the team the opportunity to send and receive this information without using the internet or any other means of transmission, which eliminated the possibility of being shut down, censored, or otherwise interfered with.

"It gets better," he explained. "I received correspondence from a billionaire businessman (for purposes of this story, we'll call Mr. X), who has his own system of satellites that he uses as an alternative to typical Internet connectivity, among other personal uses. Mr. X has offered unlimited uses of his satellite system for Mac's presidential campaign. This means that the deep state has no way whatsoever to interfere with Mac's public interface. As if that's not enough, Mr. X has put together an additional two billion dollars made up of a personal contribution and money from a few trusted colleagues of his." Mr. X explained that he was unable to disclose how he was made aware of Mac's upcoming run or his goals and background but assured Pete that it was the most amazing and game-changing thing he could imagine, and that was saying a lot for a man like this!

Mac looked over at Danie who just said, "I had no idea."

Continuing, Pete outlined, in general terms, that in addition to buying large blocks of television airtime, the team would use Mr. X's systems to broadcast through the Internet and directly to any person's phone via a new app that would allow the phone to connect directly to Mr. X's satellite system. The app-embedded software contains encryption that could not be broken by existing technology, and information transmitted would only be calculated at Mac's headquarters if received from an individual phone. This meant that the deep state could not adversely affect the data even if they used the app. They would have to use millions of individual phones to have any meaningful effect, and they would not be aware that individual reception was even a consideration because they could not access the encrypted code.

"I know that this is mind-boggling, but we have been running tests, and it's real," Pete said.

Jake said, "A game changer doesn't even begin to define the significance of this information. This means that Mac can communicate, without interference, with the entire country and receive real-time input regarding the acceptance of his platform, intent to support him at the ballot box, and, most importantly, the exact number of votes he receives. Ballot tampering efforts by the deep state could be challenged with irrefutable evidence. It's going to revolutionize voting in our country." The group fell silent, and Jake suggested that cocktails, strong ones, were in order. There were no objections.

Poor Kate was in a state of shock and had momentarily forgotten all about Mac's property, which was only a twenty-minute drive away, until Mac said, "How about heading over to view the property tomorrow morning, hon?"

"Sure," she replied.

The mood was, well, it was indescribable. Mac had a magnificent team, he had more than enough cash, he had the new advanced technology, and it seemed that the mission had become a plausible effort. The rest of the day was spent enjoying each other's company, and Kate had the chance to meet her future stepmother, which was another knockout blow to her already overburdened mind. Kate immediately loved Danie. Danie seemed to have that effect on everyone. She was remarkably likable; she just came across as genuine and humble despite her beauty and other attributes. Danie and Kate spent a lot of time and consumed many drinks while the whole Allagash Lake scenario was explained including the attraction between her and Kate's dad that had blossomed into a deep and still growing love.

Meanwhile, the men continued to talk about the implications of Mac winning the election. Jake said that a president who was not indebted to anyone and who had the integrity and resolve to gut the deep state from the top-down might just turn our divided and morally confused country back in the right direction would be like a breath of fresh air. He added that, unlike the deep state's motivation, Mac didn't want to mold the population to his own ideology. Rather, he wanted to open the door to folks returning to their natural inclination toward the importance of family, fairness, and acceptance of all others as equals. He said that people don't inherently want to be controlled, and safety and honesty would naturally usher in greater acceptance of each other without the bigotry that the deep state has been nurturing for so very long. "Sure, there would always be evil among us; that's the nature of humans, but most men, women, and children are decent individuals, and absent the behavior modification that they have been subjected to, peace and prosperity will return."

In the morning, Stan flew Jake home to Cape Cod, and Mac, Danie, Kate, and Pete went to view the home Kate had located. The driveway was lined with mature white pines and maples, and it wound close to one thousand yards from the main road to the house. The grounds were manicured meticulously and the house itself was log with an attached three-car garage. It was a two-story dwelling with the rear-facing the bay, very much like Pete's. Inside, it boasted a great room with a thirty-foot ceiling and a kitchen that would make a professional chef jealous. It had four bedrooms, four and a half baths, and a massive deck. The backyard was relatively small, positioning the house closer to the ocean. The elevation was about fifty feet, and there was an elaborate staircase that led down to the rocky beach. It was not a deep harbor situation, and a dock extended out to a depth of eight feet, which was perfect for a small boat that they would use to run out to the soon-to-be acquired seaworthy vessel (to be acquired) moored another hundred yards out in twenty-five feet of water. The small backyard boasted a beautiful, heated pool and separate hot tub, as well as a changing house and a poolside fireplace.

The $2.6 million dollar price tag wasn't for the faint of heart, but Mac and Danie decided to make the purchase anyway. Kate would receive over $80,000 in commissions. She agreed to get started on the paperwork and Mac provided contact information for his legal and finance people.

The group returned to Pete's, and Stan was already back from the Cape. Another celebratory afternoon followed. During the afternoon, Mac suggested that after a small wedding at the new house, he and Danie might take that trip to Thailand for a honeymoon. There was no argument from the bride-to-be.

Now, Mac needed to decide on a running mate in short order because many states require an announced running mate as a prerequisite to getting on their ballot as an independent. Jake had earlier suggested a close friend of his (who, for purposes of this writing, we'll call 'Mr. R'). Mr. R was a current southern governor who had become a beacon of light during the COVID-19 pandemic. His record of masterful state management often ran in direct opposition to federal mandates, producing a state whose economic and social environment had become a magnet for citizens desperately searching for a place to relocate from oppressive state-enacted overregulation, both (social and economic) as well as politically controlled law enforcement protocols.

Mac decided to go with Mr. R and contacted Jake with his decision, who agreed to make arrangements. Evidently, Jake had already broached the possibility with his friend, who tentatively agreed willingly. Mr. R would be brought into the loop with the exception that no information concerning Danie's specifics were to be released to anyone other than the small original team leaders.

Mark had been in touch recently and posed a serious concern. Considering the nature of Mac's platform, Mac would become a high probability target for elimination by any means by the deep state, and since he wasn't qualified for secret service protection, Mark suggested he assemble a significant team of ex-secret service agents and prior military professionals. It would be wildly expensive, but he considered it absolutely necessary to protect Mac during the campaign. Mac had agreed and Mark was actively establishing the protection detail.

It was decided to return to Nebraska the following morning while Kate arranged for the house purchase. Mac's legal and financial teams had the authority to close the deal without his physical presence, and Kate assured them that the cash purchase would expedite the process. She estimated they would be in their new house within two weeks.

It had been a whirlwind of a week, and by bedtime, everyone welcomed a good night's rest.

# CHAPTER 19
## BACK TO NEBRASKA AND THEN THE WEDDING

In the morning, Mac and Danie boarded the jet, and Stan flew them back to Lincoln Airport. It was another less-than-perfect morning but warm and dry. After landing, Mac and Danie headed to his golf course apartment, and Stan, after tending to the jet, planned to have a few days to relax.

Walking into his little two-bedroom apartment the whole series of recent events seemed like some kind of a dream more than reality to Mac. They had some unwind time and, like many couples, just lounged around and watched a movie in the evening.

In the morning, Danie found Mac with a coffee out on his small balcony that overlooked the small pond on the golf course. It was a beautiful morning, and she sat beside her fiancé and watched the geese with their fledgling young.

The team leaders were all actively attending to their respective assignments and all team leaders maintained constant communication with each other and Mac. Danie had never held a golf club and was excited to learn to play. Over the following two weeks, Mac and Danie spent a lot of time on the course driving range and playing the course. Mac always maintained a constant awareness of the team's progress.

Twelve days into their downtime in Lincoln, Kate called and advised that the Rockland property sale had closed and was ready for Mac and Danie. She had arranged for a local landscaper to maintain the grounds and a cleaning service to maintain the interior of the home. Meanwhile, Mac's buddy Steve, another retired air traffic controller and experienced mariner, had located a boat from his friend and agreed to captain it provided he received a couple of days' notice before trips were scheduled. Steve was a tall athletic man who had trained for and run in three iron man events which are (An Ironman Triathlon is one of a series of long-distance triathlon races organized by the World Triathlon Corporation (WTC), consisting of a 2.4-mile (3.9 km) swim, a 112-mile (180.2 km) bicycle ride and a marathon 26.22-mile (42.2 km) run completed in that order, a total of 140.6 miles (226.3 km). It is widely considered one of the most difficult one-day sporting events in the world. He had located a Wesmac 42 with a new larger transom door, a new hinged side boarding door, an angled ramp with a carbon fiber rolling base, and custom handrails. A Wesmac could not be more safe, comfortable, and accommodating to deliver more precious times on the water to her family and friends. With two U-shaped dining/seating areas, one enclosed aft with removable Isenglass curtains and the other in the climate-controlled main salon, an upper bar equipped with sink, refrigeration, and oversized counter space, "Relentless" is the perfect vessel for day use and entertaining. An oversized centerline head/sink/counter space (forward of the galley) is perfect for those who require/appreciate a space with more home-like proportions. An electric (24v) wheelchair lift has been engineered (currently in storage and off the boat) for access to the head over 3-steps down from the main salon. Crew bunks to the port of the galley are handy for boat deliveries (North & South) when the owner/guests are not aboard. A fully equipped Navigation center at the helm (to starboard) includes oversized GPS plotters interfaced with Radar, transducers, Sat weather, and more.) and assured Mac to have the boat moored at the Rockland property in a few days.

Steve also picked up a Carolina skiff to ferry folks from the dock out to the Wesmac. Like most of Mac's closest friends, Steve comes with a funny old story. Back in the early seventies, while both young men were stationed at Loring Air Force Base in Limestone, Maine, they were fishing the Madawaska stream one early spring morning. It was a warm day, but the water was still running high and cold from the spring snow melt-off. They used to joke about how they certainly couldn't catch any trout because the water was too high and too cold (mocking a common local misunderstanding). Steve had moved off the stream and was fishing up a small brook that fed into the larger stream from the east. It was a rocky brook but had some nice sandy shores that were mostly overhung by small willow trees. Steve had been up the brook, so Mac decided to follow him to see what was happening. As Mac rounded a bend in the brook, he saw Steve standing on his tiptoes with an alder branch bent over him. Steve was cussing up a storm, and Mac realized that he had his line hung in the alder branch with the very sharp number eight hook embedded in his nose. Mac burst into a belly laugh, and his buddy was not amused. "Help me get this fucking thing out of my nose, you asshole!" Steve shouted.

Mac reached up and taking the line in his hand, relieving the tension, said, "Maybe I should just let go and really set that hook."

Steve came back with, "Fuuuck Youuuu!" Mac cut the line and then, using a pair of fishing pliers, ripped the barbed piece of metal out of Steve's nose. It was one of the funniest things Mac had ever seen, and Steve swore that if Mac ever mentioned it, he would swear that it all happened in reverse, with Mac being impaled rather than him. Over the years the story had become an iconic event, with both guys talking over each other with exact opposite versions of the event whenever the two happened to be having a drink in camp or anywhere with other buddies.

The day of the news that the Rockland property was available, Mac asked Stan to have the jet ready the following morning to head back east.

During the ride to Rockland, Mark checked in by phone and explained that he had assembled a team of fifteen professionals, all prior military, and some ex-secret service, with a variety of skill sets. He said that he would like to establish a command and control/training facility on a thousand-acre ranch about forty minutes by air from his place. Mac would have preferred to have all the teams on the East Coast, but he agreed to the funding and instructed Mark to make arrangements through his accountants and legal team. Mark also informed Mac that, as a result of Mr. X's satellites, they would have real-time imaging almost equal to what the current Secret Service has. He continued that once Mac's candidacy begins to take hold and the deep state realizes that they can't interfere with broadcasts or communications from the public, the likelihood of an assignation attempt will become a serious threat. He assured Mac that his team would be up and operational to provide even better protection than the Secret Service because they had no federal red tape to restrict them, and information wouldn't be leaking. Mac was happy with the news from his old buddy, and he trusted him personally and his instincts with his life without question.

They arrived in Rockland close to noon and were met by Pete. On the ride to Mac's new home, Pete shared more good news. He had made some modifications at his place to create a secure operations center for the IT team for the duration. His four-member team was already on site, and he had arranged for a house rental nearby to house them. He explained that these were the best in their fields and that they had already built a prototype receiver that would parse (separate as needed) all messages and had written software (encoded with the new advanced technology) to generate a series of remarkable reports. The app for general download and use by the public was completed and being tested. So far, the receiver was able to parse messages that originated from a single device from spam generated by the deep state and sent from phantom locations successfully. "This technology is going to make them crazy!" he said.

They went to Pete's home first to see his new setup. He had transformed his great room (large living room) into a control center and when Mac saw it, the first thing he thought of was he had walked onto a Hollywood sci-fi set. There were control modules all connected remotely to big screen monitors like you'd expect to see in a movie, except this was real! Pete introduced his team and assured Mac their backgrounds were fully vetted, and he knew each of them personally, or they had been vetted by trusted colleagues. Even so, every person was searched, entering, and leaving so no hardware could be smuggled in or out, and, for the duration of the campaign, each team member had agreed to be surveilled 24/7 by agents provided by Mark. It sounded like overkill to Mac, but Mark had insisted, and Pete was in complete agreement. It seemed like things were really coming together.

After the introductions and quick tour were completed, Pete ran Mac and Danie over to their new home. The two had decided to furnish the place with new furniture and trimmings and Mac asked Danie if she would manage that task. She happily agreed, and Mac suggested they ask Kate to locate a sharp assistant to help his future bride with the logistics. She was happy to accept the help. The groundskeeping team (three men selected and vetted) were already at work, and the grounds looked great.

It would take a couple of weeks to get the house furnished, and Pete had arranged a cozy seaside cottage for the couple to use in the meantime. After a quick tour of the property, Pete ran Mac and Danie over to the cottage. When they arrived, they discovered that Kate had purchased, through Mac's accountants, two vehicles for them. Mac had a new Chevy pickup and Danie was presented with Chevy Tahoe for her personal use. Once again, Mac had to remind himself that this was really happening, and he wasn't dreaming.

At the cottage, Pete shares more news from Jake. It seemed that Mr. X had used his influence to secure significant blocks of TV time on all news stations, Republican and Democrat, for Mac to make his introduction speech. It was an expensive but necessary undertaking, and it was the perfect way to introduce Mac to the country and explain the new app to American voters. To activate the app, voters would be required to provide viable proof of United States citizenship. This was expected to be an issue initially, but the team believed that once the voters understood the reason for providing such proof was to prevent the deep state from interfering with the results, they would be proud to comply. For the first time, voters would have the opportunity to voice their will with full confidence it would be heard and counted. It was a powerful message and would require time and patience to be fully accepted.

The next step after the wedding was the drafting of Mac's introduction speech. Jake had instructed that he wanted Mac to write his own speech because he wanted it to be from the heart and mostly in Mac's own words. He, of course, would have a professional available to polish it, but only with Mac's approval. Mac agreed but was, again, seriously challenged emotionally.

Pete said, "I bet your head is running wild, Mac. Let's relax, down a few cocktails, and just watch the sunset." Mac agreed, but he felt as physically and emotionally drained as he had ever experienced before. Several drinks into the evening, everyone seemed to be relaxed and content once more.

The wedding was planned to happen in two weeks, which didn't give Danie and her assistant much time to furnish the large house, but Danie seemed to accept that challenge as a mission of love. The wedding was to be a small, very private event at their new home. Only the team leaders and Mac's kids were invited, and no public announcements were to be made. Mark insisted on providing security, as much of a dry run as a genuine necessity since no one knew who Mac was yet.

Neither Mac nor Danie could get to sleep easily because their minds were racing, but eventually, the soothing sound of the surf on the rocky shore lulled them into a peaceful rest.

# CHAPTER 20
## THE WEDDING, THEN THE SPEECH

It was a warm but overcast Sunday at the beginning of August when Mac and Danie formally became a team for life. The weather wasn't perfect, but at least it didn't rain. The small gathering watched as they were pronounced man and wife by a catholic priest on Mac's back lawn with a backdrop of the ocean complete with gulls and waves. They decided to keep the affair informal, so guests were in casual dress. Mac wore slacks, a dress shirt (no tie), and a sports coat, and Danie stole the show in a simple dress with her long black hair down. Even attired to be simple, she was the epitome of elegance.

The day was a wonderful success, and the newlyweds spent their wedding night in their new home but left in the morning with Stan for Nassau and a five-day honeymoon. Mac's jet, with its 3,500-mile range, was the perfect mode of travel and Mac had rented a beautiful seaside cottage on the southwest shore facing the shallow waters that were perfect for swimming and fishing. Stan brought a girlfriend to share his weeks' vacation on the islands with no arguments.

They arrived without incident, and both couples settled into their respective lodgings. Mac and Danie, although newlyweds, were already functioning as an established couple so the honeymoon was more of a break than a novelty, although Mac still tingled whenever he was close to his stunning wife.

The main topic of discussion was the content of Mac's all-important speech. They spent hours verbally addressing it, from the introduction of the candidate through outlining his platform in terms that would reciprocate with everyone, introducing the use of his new technology and why it was imperative to provide an absolute consequence for every vote, and finally addressing some of his planned initial actions aimed at gutting the Washington establishment, ensuring border security and dealing with the growing drug and violence malignancy in our country and reinstating many of President Trump's economic policies in an effort to reduce our dependency on foreign powers, reestablish our dominance in energy production, and encourage manufacturing to return stateside. No small series of statements, to be sure!

It was a perfect setting to work on the speech, free from any distractions except the regular updates from the respective team leaders.

On the morning of the fifth and last day in paradise, Mac forwarded his first draft to Jake for his review and input.

"My name is Charles McNamara; I usually answer to Mac. I'd like to take this opportunity to introduce myself and announce my candidacy for president of the United States of America. I'm a complete unknown, and I'll do my best to explain who I am and why I'm making this very difficult decision.

"I'm just a regular guy. I spent many years in the United States Air Force as an air traffic controller, I've seen combat in North Africa, I was married for nearly a quarter of a century and divorced amicably in 2003. I have a large family, and we're all close. I have been a Master Maine hunting/fishing guide and owner and operator of private businesses. I'm a pilot and have earned a Master of Business Administration in aviation management degree. After teaching for a short time and running my business software company I returned to federal law enforcement until I retired in 2003. That's me, in a nutshell, just one of you.

"Now to the crux of the matter, why am I running, and what can I do for you, the people of this great country. Like most of you, folks from all political perspectives and from all economic and ethnic backgrounds, I've watched the country that I grew up in and fought to protect be methodically broken by those few with money and power who want only to subdue and control you. We've always had different opinions on politics and economics, and that's been the beauty of this nation. We were free to disagree and make every effort to promote our preferred ideology, but we were free to pursue those things without fear of repercussions from the very government that was designed to be of the people, by the people, and for the people! A government with officials elected fairly by you and who are to serve in your best interest, not their own.

"We've had troubled times, but so has every civilization in recorded history. Humans aren't perfect creatures, and that holds true for every ethnicity, every religious inclination, and every individual personality. The thing with the United States of America is that from the first days, we have improved slowly but steadily, learning, sometimes harshly, from our mistakes. If that weren't true, then why are people from every other nation clamoring to join our society?

"Most of us have very similar interests concerning basic needs. We pray for safety, to be able to move about in our own neighborhoods or in our cities with a reasonable assurance of safety. We want to have the right to raise a family with a reasonable expectation that our neighbors or anyone else will, at the very least, not persecute us for being ourselves, provided that we return the treatment by not harassing them either. We want our kids to have the opportunity of a good education without the influence of politically motivated influence regarding matters that belong to the right of the parent. We want our kids to attend school and enjoy an educational and social experience that is positive and has the best interest of the children front and center. None of us want to be afraid to move about in our towns and cities for fear of interaction with violence from gangs or other radical individual who are heavily influenced by the few who desire control for their own purposes. We don't want to see our kids or friends being killed by drugs that are pouring across our open borders. We just want to live in peace and prosper according to our individual talents and hard work. Finally, we don't want the government that we have elected to exert increasingly unreasonable control over who we are, how we raise our families, what we eat, what we drive, or what we are allowed to say!

"There is and has been an order of elite, powerful men, and women who, without consideration of any political alignment, have been slowly using the news, social media, and our educational system to modify the nation's morality and cohesiveness. Don't confuse illegitimate rhetoric about inclusiveness and climate nonsense with their deliberate behavior modification. They want to break down the core family values and community morality. They are disarming us. They have opened the border, endangering all of us for their own purposes. They are turning us against each other and against the first responders who risk their lives every day to protect us. Not many years ago, it would have been considered child abuse to discuss gender identity with a six-year-old in school, but today, it's being mandated, and parents are blocked from having any voice in the matter. Kids in grammar school should be concerned with playing and having fun, not totally confused by matters that, under normal circumstances, would never have crossed their minds.

"I'm not going to stand here and advocate that recent elections have definitively been tampered with by this deep state, but I would ask how many of you at least worry about the value of your vote being negated by nefarious means.

"It's time to grab the reins and take back control of our country! It's not too late, but it's getting there fast. I'll address all these issues and more in appearances to come but let me provide a snapshot of what I plan to do to get things moving back in the right direction.

"I recently came into a windfall of cash that will be explained with complete transparency. I was shocked by it, and it has no ties to any political or socially driven groups. As a result, I plan to run as an independent candidate. No independent has ever launched a successful campaign, but I believe we can make it happen together. I've put together a team of technology experts who have designed hardware and software that cannot be cracked by political opponents. We've created an app that each of you can download to your phones for free. From the app, we can provide updates to my campaign that are free from being blocked or otherwise tampered with. When and if you decide to get on board and vote for me, we can provide, with your consent, an accurate tally of the votes. Your voice will matter, and you will see in real-time everything that we see. This is power, folks. You can disagree and vote your own mind, but supporters will be certain that one hundred percent of their votes are tallied and counted for the presidency and for all federal elections. It's time that our elected officials at every level become aware that you are, once again, their boss and that their job is to represent you ethically or be removed by the next vote!

"Thanks for the opportunity to at least offer, once again, under the Constitution of our country with reasonable confidence, that our voices are collectively heard, and our desires represented by the officials we choose by voting to serve us. I'll give you time to digest my introduction and promise to return with much greater details about how I plan to turn the tide in United States politics. My app is called "DTM" (Don't Tread on Me), and it's available at no cost on Google apps, you can email my campaign at DTM.com, and we'll make it available to you immediately. I gave this a lot of thought, and although there is a segment of the nation who will express offense, I believe that it accurately represents the vast majority of us who have had enough of government by and for the government. Don't tread on me began on what's known as the Gadsden flag, which features a rattlesnake coiled above the expression on a yellow background. The flag was first flown on a warship in 1775 as a battle cry for American independence from British rule. It's credited to Christopher Gadsden, a soldier and politician from South Carolina.

"The snake was an established symbol for America at the time. Benjamin Franklin notably used it, saying the rattlesnake never backed down when provoked, which captured 'the temper and conduct of America.'

"The tread in Gadsden's defiant phrase, 'don't tread on me,' means 'to step, walk, or trample so as to press, crush, or injure something.' And so, with its tongue flicked, fangs out, and body coiled in defense, the rattlesnake and motto warns: 'If you dare put your foot down on me, I will strike.'

"God bless the United States of America!"

Over the next few days, every one of the team leaders (by Zoom calls) agreed with the introduction speech, and Jake added the suggested next steps in the campaign process. The day before they were to return to Maine, Jake called in to inform Mac that the arrangements for the public broadcast were complete, and the announcement was scheduled to be aired on the following Monday during prime time on all major media outlets. He also arranged to have 200 local television stations air the announcement the same day. Additionally, he booked airtime on a multitude of radio stations across the country. It was dearly expensive, but he suggested it was necessary to kick-start the campaign and provide an initial reaction.

# CHAPTER 21
## THE CAMPAIGN AIRS

The big day arrived, and Mac's announcement hit the air at 1000 on all the major news shows and hundreds of local news and radio stations. Mac and Danie were having lunch on their new deck at 1300. when Pete arrived with news. He brought his laptop computer that contained the receiver program that analyzed all the data being received from the DTM app.

He told them that the news of Mac's announcement of his candidacy was going viral on the Internet and that more than fifty million copies of the DTM app had already been downloaded to private phones. He said that his team expects, based on the initial reaction, that close to seventy percent of the voting population might download and use the app. Some of his team expect closer to eighty percent.

"I wonder how long it will take the deep state to cancel us on left-wing news media and the Internet?" Pete asked aloud. He went on to discuss the fact that cancellation is anticipated but based on the initial download stats for the app, they will have no power to interfere with Mac's ability to communicate with most of the country. "This is great news, but, Mac, it's dangerous stuff. When the deep state loses the ability to influence a candidate and, more so, to influence the populus, they become afraid and will go to absolutely any length to regain control. We need to get Mark and his boys involved immediately!" Mac asked him if he seriously feared physical repercussions, and Pete answered, "What happened to President Kennedy and Bobby when they threatened to disband the CIA back in 1963?" That was a sobering statement, and Mac put in a call to Mark right away.

Within minutes, Mac had all team leaders on a conference call, with Mark taking the lead after Pete explained his concerns. Mark told the group that his team had already anticipated the reaction of the deep state and suggested that he establish a command post in the Rockland area immediately and get his entire team situated there. He went on to explain that he would need access to Mac's jet and a couple of helicopters for deployment and surveillance purposes. He explained that he had access to a couple of Apaches, but they weren't cheap, and he needed current pilots as well. Mac approved all of Mark's requests and contacted his daughter to find an appropriate location in town. Pete said that he was in the process of establishing the satellite visual reconnaissance through Mr. X, and his team would have new 'real-time' imagery available to Mark's guys in a day or two.

"Do you really believe that they'll go to those extreme lengths to silence Mac?" Danie asked. Mark replied that, in his experience, powerful men with nefarious agendas are not to be taken lightly, but he added that his guys were the best of the best and all 100 percent loyal and trustworthy.

"Exactly how trustworthy?" Pete asked.

"I trust each of them with my life!" was his response. That was good enough for everyone. "We can't even count on the Secret Service or the FBI," Mark added. "The agents are, for the most part, stand-up folks just doing their jobs, but I don't trust any government agency completely. We're on our own this time!" he concluded.

By early evening, the number of DTM downloads was becoming unbelievable. Nearly 175 million copies were now on private phones. Before calling it an evening, Pete said that he and Jim would begin providing updates and other pertinent information to the public through the app in the following days. He explained that the app was written to be very simple to use, which meant that more people might make an effort to submit information. "This is a game-changing tool, Mac!" he said as he left the deck.

Four days later, Kate had arranged for a nice farmhouse nearby, and Stan had picked up Mark and his team in a leased Cessna 408 Sky Courier capable of carrying nineteen passengers, and Mac met them at the airport with a rented bus for transport to the command post. He would leave arranging for Mac's team's vehicle needs to Mark. When they arrived at the command post, Mark was pleased. There was a large, mowed area where the chopper could land and take off, and the house had four bedrooms and a large living room that would become his physical command post. The team members not housed at the command post were provided rooms at a nearby motel. These guys would have been satisfied with a tent and a cot.

Mark told Mac that it would take a few days to get completely set up, and in the meantime, he and the other team leaders would be monitoring the online activity. Mac had arranged for a Zoom conference (Zoom Phone is a feature-rich cloud phone system for businesses of all sizes. It's simple to deploy and use on a mobile device, desktop, or desk phone. It pairs traditional PBX features with intelligent call routing, IVR, call recording, shared lines, and more to give you a robust VoIP phone system.) to be attended by all team leaders twice daily at 0800 EST and 1500 EST.

It didn't take long, two days later at 1500 hours (At first glance, a military time chart may appear complicated. However, it's built on a simple principle – counting the hours from 0 to 24. The day starts at 0000, referred to as 'zero hundred hours,' and ends at 2400 or 'twenty-four hundred hours. In the military time chart, the hours from midnight to noon (0000 to 1200) are the same as those in standard time, except that leading zeros are always written out. After noon, instead of resetting to 1 as in the 12-hour clock, the hours continue from 13 to 24.) Pete informed the team that the dark state had blocked all mention of Mac's campaign on left-wing news media and the Internet, citing that it was considered dangerous anti-government propaganda. The good news was that the millions of DTM users were recognizing the fact that they couldn't access any information online and were steadfast in continuing with DTM. Pete added that, apparently, the deep state had already attempted to access the satellites with no success, and he was certain they would be unable to hack into the advanced code used to generate the app. All the data was being received and parsed by the receiver designed by Pete's people. Jim had prepared a statement addressing the interference by the deep state and pledged that all users would continue to receive updates through the app and that their votes would be irrefutably counted on the day.

Mark interjected and explained that this was serious stuff and that, in his experience, once the deep state recognized that a threat, they could not control was gaining steam, they would take any action, including physical elimination. Assassination (assignation) was on the table. He added that his team was ready and able to act when required. He told everyone that he was up and monitoring online chatter and 'otherwise monitoring' (hacking) individual and corporate text, email, and phone conversations. Additionally, with the immeasurable assistance from Mr. X, they were able to perform satellite imagery monitoring of suspicious activities.

Over the following two weeks, the number of DTM users continued to climb, and the only sympathetic major news station, Box News (we'll call it BOX NEWS), was covering the sudden lack of coverage by mainstream media and posting updates by Mac's team including instructions for downloading the DTM app. The number of downloads now exceeded 200 million. That exceeded sixty percent of the population, let alone the voting populus.

During the fifth week following Mac's candidacy announcement, Mark and Pete identified a credible threat associated with the deep state. For purposes of this writing, we'll identify the principal U.S. threat as 'DS-1' and an affiliated foreign threat as 'DS-2'. DS-1 was identified as senior leadership in several government agencies, and DS-2 as a group of senior foreign government agencies and private individuals. Although the 'surveillance' by Mac's team was technically questionable with respect to legality, they all felt that desperate times warranted desperate actions. "Does this mean that Mac's life might actually be in danger?" Danie asked, and Mark said, "We're all in danger, hon!"

The intel being gathered seemed to suggest that the threat was in the initial stages. The enemy (DS-1 and DS-2) realized they were facing something unexpected and something that they couldn't control. There was much chatter about their inability to access the satellites or the app code, and that frightened them. Added to that, Box News was reporting the remarkable acceptance of the DTM app and had run editorials about how, for the first time in history, Americans' voices were being heard without interference from the deep state.

Mark had begun running training operations that closely resembled a combination of a secret service protection detail and a covert operation conducted by JSOC operatives. What this means is Mark's team has all the capabilities and expertise of the Secret Service, but they also operate as a black operation. A black operation or black ops is a covert or clandestine operation by a government agency, a military unit, or a paramilitary organization; it can include activities by private companies or groups. Key features of a black operation are its secrecy, and it is not attributable to the organization carrying it out.

A single such activity may be called a black bag operation; that term is primarily used for covert or clandestine surreptitious entries into structures to obtain information for human intelligence operations. Such operations have been conducted by the FBI, CIA, KGB, Mossad, MI6, MI5, ASIS, COMANF, DGSE, AISE, CNI, MSS, R&AW, DGFI, SVR, FSB, Kuwait 25th Commando Brigade, ISI, and the intelligence services of other states. The main difference between a black operation and one that is merely secret is that a black operation involves a significant degree of deception to conceal who is behind it or to make it appear that some other entity is responsible. This makes them a very dangerous enemy.

Two weeks later, Mark reported that the extent of the suspect threat was more expansive than originally assessed and requested to engage more men and additional funding for his operations. Mac agreed without hesitation.

Another week passed, and Mac was slated to appear live on Box News again to address the American public. Mark told the team leaders that the deep state had identified Mac's home, and they were surveilling open communications. The good news was that Mac's team only used open communications to insert disinformation aimed at confusing the deep state, and all real communications were made through the advanced encrypted software provided by Danie's team.

Evidently, the deep state had decided that an attack at Mac's home was too risky, and it was suggested that an assassination in a public place, similar to the JFK assassination, could be managed in a way to place the blame on a scapegoat like Lee Harvey Oswald in 1963.

Mac's team leaked detailed communications describing the exact route he would take for his appearance on Fox News. It included travel by his jet to New York and then the exact route by vehicle to the Box News headquarters.

The deep state took the bait, and Mark's team learned that the hit would occur at JFK International Airport when Mac exited to enter his vehicle. Since Mac was arriving by private jet, he would not be passing through the main terminal. Instead, he would be arriving and departing from the general aviation terminal, which has significantly less traffic than the main terminals. The deep state planned to make the hit by means of a terrorist jihadist bomber (a jihadist recruited and misinformed by them who is willing to sacrifice his life for the cause) that would detonate the bomb immediately adjacent to Mac's vehicle. This tactic would eliminate Mac and protect the deep state from the wild media coverage of a random attack on U.S. soil.

Mark had provided the description and license plate through his disinformation campaign, and the deep state swallowed it completely. Mark had established his team as a licensed personal protection agency and complied with all training requirements. This meant that they were licensed to conduct surveillance and carry fully automatic weapons in the performance of their duties. He had obtained the deep state's information on the bomber and the vehicle to be used.

The day arrived and Mac's whole team was on full alert. Mac and his immediate entourage left Rockland and landed at the general aviation facility at JFK on time and as scheduled. Mark's team was in place with three vehicles on the ground carrying ten fully armed operatives and computer links to live satellite coverage e (and fortunately the weather was clear) as well as live chatter from DS-1 And DS-2 components. Fortunately, the weather was clear. Mark alerted everyone that he had eyes on the Suburban carrying the bomb and he planned to intercept it well short of where Mac was to enter his vehicle. Mark had four of his shooters located right by Mac's vehicle just in case of a problem intercepting the bomber. Mark knew that the bomb was to be detonated by the bomber himself, so it was impossible to stop the vehicle and defuse the situation. The plan was to make three simultaneous kill shots from different angles that would kill the bomber immediately and eliminate the threat to nearby civilians. His team couldn't provide evidence of DS-1 and DS-2 involvement, so this was to be a covert operation with immediate extraction after the shots to avoid detection.

The Suburban approached within one-quarter of a mile, and when it reached the designated interception point, Mak called the shot! Almost simultaneously, three silenced .308 caliber carbine rifles barked, and the bomber's head simply exploded. The vehicle was only traveling at about five miles per hour and harmlessly edged into the curb and stopped. Mark's team was long gone before any police arrived. At the exact same time, five other leading characters from DS-1 and DS-2 were taken down. Three by long-range rifle fire and two by a helicopter launched AIM-92 Stinger missiles while they were traveling in a private jet in South America. The deep state couldn't make the hits public and was forced to suck it up, but the message sent was clear as day "You're fucking with forces that you can't control—stand down!"

Mac's vehicles were able to depart the airport and arrive at Box News headquarters as planned. When the interview was filmed, the news of the terrorist attack was being broadcast. Mac addressed America and suggested that such attacks were horrific and said that the perception of American strength financially and militarily would be returned under his presidency and that would make bad actors think twice before engaging the United States of America in the future.

He continued to further detail his views on the dangerous and powerful influence the deep state has in the world and the extent to which the real voice of the American people has been muted. He discussed the fact that radical elements are granted not only a voice but praise from the mainstream media, who are controlled by the deep state. Mac further discussed the open border situation in our country. He asked folks to consider exactly why the current administration rescinded the prior president's strong immigration controls in favor of a policy that encourages people, many of whom come from countries hostile to the United States, to enter America illegally, anticipating being rewarded for committing a crime. I (remember illegal entry is a crime no matter how you dress it up. He proposed that the administration, in cooperation with the deep state, had violated the Constitution of the United States of America by deliberately ushering in millions of criminals and nurturing them to broaden a voter base that they could control. Ultimately this plan postures the left-wing politicians as monarchs more than leaders.

He finished by explaining that he has provided the nation with the first un-hackable tool that provides true freedom of speech and a means of insuring the voice of all is heard!

The response to his interview, according to Box News and data collected from the DTM app, was remarkable. People were coming together, and Mac's popularity was growing fast.

Back at Mac's home, the team leaders' first Zoom meeting after the assassination attempt was both exuberant and cautious. Mark reported that DS-1 and DS-2 chatter was wild and indicated they were completely taken by surprise and confused by Mac's ability to circumnavigate their deeply embedded network of spies and well-placed politicians and civilians. He reiterated that since the deep state was unable to control Mac's interaction with the population, Mac had become a target of opportunity because, by their reasoning, if you can't control the narrative, then eliminate it by any means possible.

Mark, then, offered a note of consolation. He told the team that until Mac's assumption of the office of the president and gaining control, the threat would be deadly serious, but the plan to strike the gangs and drug cartels immediately would change the dynamic quickly. When the deep state saw Mac eliminate the threat within our borders and the supporting elements abroad through surgical kinetic strikes, respect in the form of fear would give them serious pause. He concluded that without the advanced technology provided by Danie, none of this could be accomplished.

# CHAPTER 22
## THE CAMPAIGN CONTINUES

Over the rest of the campaign, Mac's popularity grew and the input from the DTM app was refined even more by Pete's great IT team. The deep state never stopped trying to hack Mac's satellite links or to break the code that drives the DTM app with no success. They attacked Mac's campaign relentlessly through the mainstream media they controlled. As support groups began to appear for Mac, Democrat-controlled states, under the guise of protecting law-abiding citizens, used their law enforcement and court power to disrupt, halt, and intimidate the supporters. It became a fierce effort to prevent this previously unknown independent candidate from running. It was so severe that the incumbent president and the GOP nominee were receiving less news time than Mac was. Unfortunately, except for Box News, all of Mac's coverage was negative.

The deep state searched relentlessly for dirt on Mac or Danie, but he just didn't have any skeletons in his closet. He was an open book with nothing but honorable service in uniform, private business endeavors with only the highest level of integrity, and finally, honorable federal service until he retired from Homeland Security. It must have been maddening for the deep state to find no dirt and more frustrating to see that all their disinformation efforts were falling on deaf ears as

Americans flocked to what had clearly become a return to morality and escape from being controlled by the government. It became evident that people were excited by regaining confidence that their voices would be heard and attended to by the politicians they elected to represent their safety and desires.

Time was flying by, and the day of reckoning—Election Day—was only two months away. At an afternoon Zoom meeting, Mark reported that another assassination attempt was being planned. The deep state was taking much better precautions to protect their electronic chatter, but Pete and Mark's team was always one step ahead with regard to physical and electronic surveillance. Danie's advanced technology continued to protect Mac's communications completely.

Mark told the team leaders that, in an act of total desperation, they decided to hit Mac's house when he was at home. This was an escalation like nothing that has ever been attempted, but they felt that, again, the blame could be placed on a terrorist organization. The plan was to launch an R-29RM Shtil missel (The R-29RM Shtil (Russian: Штиль, lit. "Calmness," NATO reporting name SS-N-23 Skiff), is a liquid propellant, submarine-launched ballistic missile in use by the Russian Navy. It had the alternate Russian designations RSM-54 and GRAU index 3M27. It was designed to be launched from the Delta IV submarine, each of which is capable of carrying sixteen missiles. The R-29RM could carry four 100-kiloton warheads and had a range of about 8,500 kilometers (5,300 mi) from a submarine some 1,200 miles off the Maine coast. The submarine would be reported to be scrapped by the Russian Navy and acquired and reconditioned by an extremist group.

Mark explained that he put out feelers at the highest level of government to see if a black op would be sanctioned to prevent such a hypothetical attack on U.S. soil. When the suggested target was identified as Mac, the president directly intervened and squashed the idea. He said that it was a waste of time to entertain hypothetical scenarios that weren't brought to him with hard evidence. Then, privately, he was overheard chastising his senior advisers for even suggesting such an operation and further instructed senior intelligence agency directors to consider Mac as a possible national security threat and approved a deep dive into his background and current activities to produce sufficient evidence to support action against him. In other words, the deep state's spokesman made it perfectly clear that Mac was to be considered a threat to them and dealt with accordingly.

"So, if we can't count on support from any military contacts, how in the holy fuck do we stop this one?" Mac asked. Pete interrupted by suggesting that with the help of Danie's advanced software, perhaps his programmers, working with Mark's ex-military operatives, might be able to hack into the sub's communications and, more specifically, into the electronic arming and detonation commands inside the missiles. Mark said that, like the first assassination attempt, they could feed misinformation to DS-1 and DS-2 operators and give them a date and time that Mac and Danie would be at the Rockland home. Time was critical because there were only six weeks to the election.

Four days later, at the morning Zoom conference, Pete and Mark were center stage. Pete's team had designed a hacking program with the help of Mark's ex-navy commander, and they were successful at gaining access to two Russian subs without detection. Mark added they could now initiate self-destruction of missiles from an airborne transmitter.

Mac okayed Mark to put out the disinformation and make it clear that he and Danie would only be at home the following weekend and that they would be traveling thereafter right up to election night.

The deep state again took the bait immediately, and chatter indicated that the sub would be in position only 500 miles offshore and would launch the attack at 0100 on the upcoming Saturday. Pete had developed a portable hacking and hardware that operated exclusively with their new advanced code. Pete, Mark, and Mark's sub-expert would fly with Stan on Mac's jet to stop the attack.

Although the deep state couldn't intercept any of Mac's encrypted communications and believed that what they were receiving was genuine, they did have full access to military and intelligence satellites that gave them real-time visual confirmation of Mac and Danie's movements. Mark wouldn't hear about Mac being at home the weekend of the proposed attack and he arranged to make a swap during a fishing trip with one of his men and a woman fitting Danie's description. The two decoys would be below deck a full day before the fishing trip, and the deep state would observe the decoys of Mac and Danie leave the house on the Friday before the attack and leave the boat (except it was the decoys) that evening.

Stan had the jet down in Virginia, which was not uncommon, and the attack prevention team was already at Mason's Virginia ranch. So, it was all set, and the chatter didn't indicate that the deep state had any idea what was going to happen. The sub reported to be near the launch coordinates and confirmed that they would be ready to launch at 0100. Stan was airborne with the team and close to a range that assured perfect communications interception. Mark ordered that the detonation would occur only as the launch hatch was opened to fire the missile. This was to provide hard evidence that the attack had been initiated just in case of an unforeseen SNAFU (military term for situation normal, all fucked up). The tension on the jet and at Mark's command post was palpable. At 1255, the order was given to launch, and at 1258, the launch doors opened. Simultaneously, Mark ordered the self-destruction activation. The missile detonated in the launch chamber, and the explosion caused catastrophic damage to the sub, which was sent to its watery grave more than 2,000 feet deep. Since the explosion was underwater approximately fifty feet and 500 miles offshore, only the operators were aware that the sub was sunk, and they certainly weren't going to make a public issue about a botched attack.

The chatter intercepted by Pete's team was amazing! DS-1 and DS-2 were completely stunned. They knew that the attack was intercepted, but they also were aware that it wasn't accomplished by any United States military or intelligence operatives because they were under the control of the deep state. The fact that there was someone or something protecting Mac that they continually failed to identify was horrifying to them.

The following morning, Mac, Danie, and all team leaders met at Mac's house, and after the celebratory discussions were finished (which took several hours and many cocktails), they returned to monitoring the data from DTM. Mac's live appearances on Box News and his hundreds of live town halls across the country, combined with his messages transmitted through DTM, had excited and united the country like nothing before had. Even 9-11 hadn't touched such a mass mix of citizens. Everyone was requested to report who they voted for on election day, and the vast majority agreed. Mac had successfully sold the idea that, with the voluntary information provided by the voters, their voices would be heard without interference by the deep state. If ballot tampering by the deep state was accomplished by altering the vote tally at electronic voting stations, Pete's data was a tool that could be presented to prove unequivocally the number of voters who voted for Mac. That information had been leaked to the deep state by Pete's team, who were now taking Mac very seriously!

This was going to be an election by the people and for the best interest of the people.

# CHAPTER 23
## THE ELECTION

Tuesday, November 5, 2024, finally arrived, and Mac's whole team was gathered at his place, watching the election progress. As afternoon morphed into evening, the results were staggering. Mac was in a commanding lead by double digits, edging out both the Republican and Democratic candidates. The mainstream media was in a frenzy because no one associated with the deep state expected this independent to actually turn the tide in an American election, especially considering the massive anti-Mac campaign presented by the mainstream media.

Pete had set up a live presentation on a big screen at Mac's house, and he was airing real time chatter by deep state actors that had been identified and intercepted and the election results at the same time.

By 2330, the new media had called the election for Mac. On Box News, it was a happy, exciting time, but on the mainstream media, it was being treated like something horrible had happened to the country. They were reporting suspicion of ballot tampering, and they just kept repeating the same talking points all night. In the morning, the election was over. Of course, the election wasn't officially over until it was certified by Congress. Election Day is typically the end of the contentious fight for the White House, but it could just be the beginning.

With both Democrats and Republicans preparing for possible legal fights over the vote count, the post-election process for seating the winner is getting a closer look.

The two-plus months of often ignored procedural steps are laid out by the U.S. Constitution and federal law, and they're far more complicated than simply handing over the keys to the White House to the winner. But generally, the president-elect gives his victory speech within a few days.

This 2024 election was unlike anything since George Washington was elected president as an independent candidate. Despite the wild excitement by the majority of the voters, demonstrations and threats of revolution were taking the main stage in mainstream media. Mac had won by a landslide, and the GOP candidate called and conceded the night of the election. The incumbent Democrat refused to concede, claiming election interference. There would be significant turmoil until Congress finally certified the election, but Mac aired his victory address on Box News on November 6. His victory speech received almost no coverage by the stunned mainstream media.

He appeared with Danie and Mr. R by his side and said,

> *"I want my first words to express my gratitude to all the citizens of the United States of America who have trusted me with the charge of leading the greatest nation on Earth! You have elected me, and it's you who I will serve with every ounce of strength in my body and soul.*

*You can expect a rough transition, folks. We have sent a warning shot across the figurative bow of the established politicians. Throughout my campaign, I've been communicating with you through limited television coverage but primarily through the Don't Tread on Me app that my team developed to eliminate interference by those who fear an administration that owes nobody favors, that has vowed to lead, according to the Constitution of our country, and that is determined to return the voice of the citizens of our country to the voice that must be heard and complied with by all elected officials. Change won't happen overnight. Like anything worthwhile, it will take time and cause some pain, but it will happen!*

*Throughout my campaign, I've been explaining what I perceive as inherently wrong in our country, and I guess that since you have elected me a vast majority of you agree with me. I want to take a few minutes to outline, clearly and unmistakably, the problems that I plan to address and how I plan to address them. I want you to hold me to my promises with the same fervor that I will hold your confidence in me as my most treasured gift and most serious responsibility to live up to.*

*Right out of the gate I will make changes to return the United States to energy independence. On day one, I'll eliminate the executive orders and policy mandates so that energy companies will once again expand their resource recovery efforts and invest heavily in new and better refinery facilities. We have the resources, and it's about time that we use them and return to a position of leadership rather than dependence on foreign players.*

*I want everyone to understand that I don't oppose research into alternative energy sources. I believe that it's our responsibility to always seek improved methods of providing energy, but let's do this like reasonable adults and recognize that change doesn't occur overnight and that mandating unrealistic goals is a ridiculous program that was designed to serve only the very few and disregard the vast majority. That is going to stop and stop fast!*

*On the same day, I will address the physical and emotional safety of all American citizens. There are a few critical issues that must be dealt with immediately. Our open border policy that has not only allowed but encouraged millions of people to enter the country illegally will end! I want to explain that it's not a question of not having empathy for people who simply want a better life. Rather, it's a matter of sovereign protection. No other nation on the planet tolerates illegal entry into their country, and this is reasonable. Countries, including ours, have immigration laws to protect the existing citizens and legal immigrants present on approved visas or paroles. The past administration opened the borders willfully and ignored existing laws and regulations in an effort to flood the country with a new population base that they intended to control. Here's the bottom line, illegal is illegal, no matter how you dice it. Illegal entry into our country is a crime, and it will be dealt with as a crime from my first day in office. Immigration and Customs Enforcement (ICE) and Border Patrol will be unshackled from adhering to administration policies and returned to the duties and authorities entrusted to them by law. We have millions of known 'gotaways' in this country thanks to the open-door policies of the prior administration, and these people didn't evade an encounter at the border for no reason.*

*In order to administer corrective actions regarding immigration issues, the directors of the FBI, Homeland Security, the CIA, the NSA, the DIA, and DOJ will be replaced by men or women, and yes, I said men or women because I can identify either quite clearly, who have come up through the ranks in their respective fields and have demonstrated the skills and integrity required to lead these agencies. None will be arbitrarily appointed because of campaign donations or affiliations with influential people. You come into play with this decision, my fellow Americans. You must make an effort to write to and call your congressional representatives and, in no uncertain terms, make them understand that political bias with respect to their support for recommended directors will not be tolerated, and if they persist with the current partisan approach, they are in their final term in office. I will uphold my promises to you, and I ask you to uphold your responsibility by using the voice that you have earned to bring Congress into check. Not a single member of my cabinet will be placed based on race, gender, political position, affiliation to anyone, or anything. They will be selected by skills and demonstrated integrity.*

*This brings me to the next issue that demands immediate correction. Gang and coordinated violence will be stopped! I will declare individuals and their support organizations domestic terrorists. As such, it opens the door to me using the full power of our great military and intelligence community to surgically strike and eliminate these threats. You all have the right to expect reasonable safety in your homes, on our streets, and in our towns and cities. I will send a message to these criminals that will raise loud criticism here at home and abroad, but I assure you that with the might of the United States unleashed in responsible and controlled action, all bad actors will be forced to reconsider engaging with us anymore. We'll take tremendous criticism from the mainstream media for a while, but they are the loud minority, and you are the powerful majority. Remember, acting together without regard to any of the biases that have torn us apart benefits everyone. I'll say it once more, it will take time, but as safety and security return to the norm, we'll learn to embrace each other as neighbors. There will always be tensions, hell we're humans, and humans aren't the most noble of creatures, but we are intelligent enough to recognize feeling safe and secure, and that's the start of breaking down social barriers.*

*Next, the matter of security of our physical and cyber infrastructure. This is a tough one, and I will get nowhere until we replace the aforementioned directors. Our agencies and the Joint Chiefs of Staff must be directed by competent individuals with unbiased positions and proven track records that bear out their integrity. This is a major safety and security issue. Think about it, do you suppose that, for example, China wants to physically destroy the United States? Of course not, and that's because they are so heavily invested in the economies of our countries. They're our enemy for sure, but they aren't foolish. What we should be concerned about is the threat of them causing a breakdown in the American way of life. If they can cause our population, out of fear, to turn on each other then they have an avenue to step in and assume control. Consider how fast people will go feral to do anything to satisfy basic needs if they are suddenly without power, fuel, food, and water. Can it happen? Absolutely! An adversarial player can interfere with our power grid by either a physical attack or, more likely, by a cyber-attack. Such a cyber-attack could shut down the financial sector and the power grid simultaneously. We need to get away from the vulnerability of foreign nations for critical materials and cyber technology. We must, and we will power up our efforts to secure ourselves and impress bad actors that the United States of America is once again the most powerful, the most stable, and the most fair nation in the world! I hate to say it, but a little fear goes a long way toward respect.*

*There are many more specific issues that we will address together, but in closing, I want to address the matter of morality and the value of family. Your government has, for a very long time, been pushing the rights and responsibilities of the parents to the side. Our educational facilities are going to be brought back to reality! Children are not going to be influenced about matters like gender identity by individuals outside the immediate family. Elementary school kids should be learning basic educational fundamentals like math, reading, and honest history in school. They need to be interested in playing and engaging in that all-too-difficult effort of learning to socialize with other children and adults. Morality, faith, and integrity, albeit supported softly at school, should and will be the responsibility of their parents.*

*I've said a lot, my friends, and you are my friends. We have some very difficult work to get done in the weeks and months to come. I said 'we' because neither of us can accomplish these goals alone. Your government needs your unrelenting support, as you deserve its support for you. We all need to recognize each other as neighbors, and having come together in this election, I believe we can do it. Our currency is printed with the term, 'In God we Trust,' so let's actually adhere to that ideology in as much as we assure every citizen the right to worship or not worship as they see fit, provided that aggression against fellow citizens isn't undertaken in the name of religion. Let's return to a reasonable moral compass. It's not that tough. The pathway is in each and every citizen's heart if they look deep enough. Let's start this journey together and remember that your neighbor, or the person down the street, basically wants what you want, which is to be safe, happy, and financially able to provide for their family. If we all, and I mean me too, just try to approach every day with that in mind, there is absolutely nothing that we can't accomplish together!*

*Thank you again, and God bless the United States of America!"*

## *The Beginning*

# ABOUT THE AUTHOR

John M. Hamilton was born in Worcester, Massachusetts and raised in the small town of Millbury. From his early days he was an avid hunter and fisherman. He briefly attended St. Benedicts College in Atchison Kansas but quit after only one semester.

He worked, for a short time as a carpenter and then a truck driver but soon enlisted in the United States Air Force and was selected to train as an Air Traffic Controller (ATC). After completing his basic ATC course in Biloxi, Mississippi, he was stationed to Loring Air Force Base in Limestone Maine. Here, he completed his training and earned a full Radar Approach Control rating. At the same time, he began his college studies taking night classes. He found his niche in northern Maine and under the tutelage of a few seasoned backwoods hunters and fisherman he flourished as an outdoorsman and earned a Master Maine Guide license.

He was reassigned to The United Kingdom in 1976 and spent three years working as an Air Traffic Controller. During that deployment he was selected for a classified deployment supporting Operation Eagle Claw (The Iranian Hostage recover mission).

He returned to Loring Air Force Base in the fall of 1980 and continued with evening college courses earning an Associate of Air

Traffic Control, a Bachelor of Professional Aeronautics, and a Master of Business Administration in Aviation degrees from Embry-Riddle Aeronautical University. He went on to teach as an adjunct professor for several years while continuing his ATC career in addition to earning his private pilot license and building over 1,200 hours as pilot in command. He also continued his lifelong love of the outdoors, becoming a long-line trapper and wilderness hunter.

He resigned from the Air Force in 1990 to pursue a business venture that earned him a global patent for an in-vessel composting reactor that he invented and built. He then turned to business software development and spent the next ten years writing software for the State of Maine including their statewide purchases program that he converted from a mainframe application to a PC based system.

In 2004 he was selected to attend The Federal Law Enforcement Training Center (FLETC) where he graduated in the first class that combined customs and immigrations officer positions. He was posted in Montana and became fully certified but resigned shortly afterwards for personal reasons.

He lived on Cape Cod, Massachusetts for several years where he worked as a commercial fisherman with his long-time friend until he returned to The Department of Homeland Security as a data analyst in St. Albans, Vermont. Two years after accepting the analyst position, he elected to return to law enforcement as an Immigrations Officer. He was posted to Lincoln, Nebraska and worked there until he retired in 2021.

After retiring he became licensed as a plain clothes investigator by the State of Nebraska and continued this work until 2024.

He's now fully retired and is devoting his time and energy to writing, golf and his continuing passion for hunting and fishing.

Printed in the USA
CPSIA information can be obtained
at www.ICGtesting.com
LVHW050732081224
798393LV00021B/275